HANG 'EM HIGH

Tucker felt the cold nudge of a Winchester muzzle against his back, shoving him forward. Reluctantly he moved, the gunmen steering him and his partners toward the stable on the other side of the clearing.

The stable was dark and smelled of hay and horse manure. Granger stared up toward the massive rafters that arched across the top of the building. Finding the one he thought best located for the hanging, he ordered a rope thrown across it.

Granger tied the knot himself, pulling it tight and leaving it to dangle. Granger's men pulled a wagon up beneath the rope, adjusted the noose, and tied off the other end. Hitching a mule to the wagon tongue, they looked to Granger for further directions.

"We'll take 'em one at a time," the rancher said.

Bantam Books by Cameron Judd
Ask your bookseller for the books you have missed

CORRIGAN

Cameron Judd

BANTAM BOOKS
NEW YORK · TORONTO · LONDON · SYDNEY · AUCKLAND

CORRIGAN

*A Bantam Book / published by arrangement with
the author*

PRINTING HISTORY
Bantam edition / August 1989

ISBN 0-553-28204-2

Published simultaneously in the United States and Canada

*Bantam Books are published by Bantam Books, a division of Bantam
Doubleday Dell Publishing Group, Inc. Its trademark, consisting of the
words "Bantam Books" and the portrayal of a rooster, is Registered in U.S.
Patent and Trademark Office and in other countries. Marca Registrada.
Bantam Books, 666 Fifth Avenue, New York, New York 10103.*

PRINTED IN THE UNITED STATES OF AMERICA

O   0 9 8 7 6 5 4 3

CORRIGAN

Chapter 1

Tucker Corrigan could see that his mother was trying hard not to cry when she came out of the back room where his father lay dying. She called him aside, away from the others.

"Tucker, your pa wants to see Jack one last time. I want you to go get him."

Tucker felt the skin on the back of his neck tighten. "But Ma, you know . . ."

"I know. But your pa needs to see his boy. I want to see him, too. You're the only one who can get him."

"What about Thurston Russell?"

"Don't you think I know the danger, Tucker? I haven't gone without seeing my oldest boy for seven years without good reason. But we can't worry about Russell this time. Your pa needs to see his son before he dies."

"When do you want me to leave?"

"First light. Jack ain't that far off, but there ain't no way to say how long your pa has. You'll have to find him and bring him home just as quick as you can."

"What if he don't want to come? He knows Russell will try to kill him."

"He'll come, no matter what, when he finds out his pa needs him."

She moved away then, leaving Tucker alone with his thoughts. He couldn't blame Pa for wanting to see Jack. It had been with Jack that Pa had come to Wyoming years ago and established a spread near the Crazy Woman Creek. Tucker had been just a little sprout then, doing most of his growing right here on the ranch. Pa had a good knowledge of the cattle business—he had worked with cattle all of his days—but knowledge and skill weren't much if a man didn't have luck.

Luck and wealth had evaded Pa throughout his life. It didn't seem fair that Pa had to lay dying with his hopes unfulfilled.

"Don't worry, Bess. This old log home ain't nothing but temporary," he had said. "In just a couple of years I'll build you a nice place, one you can be proud of."

Those years had come and gone many times over, and the new house never came into existence. Bad luck seemed to rob the Corrigans of any bit of wealth they might accumulate. When the cattle weren't dying, they were being stolen by competing ranchers or Indians. Now Danver Corrigan was on his deathbed. It wasn't fair. But Tucker had learned long ago that life for a struggling Wyoming ranching family was often a long way from fair.

If Pa had never achieved wealth, at least he had a good family. There was Jack, Tucker, Bob, Cindy, Tara, then little Benjamin Elrod. They were a good family, hardworking and God-fearing, though a bit lively and high-spirited, occasionally too much so for their own good.

Jack had been the wildest of the bunch, often taking part in games of poker at Scudder's Saloon, an institution of low repute situated in the middle of nowhere. It was a log building backed by a slightly larger building where Mel Scudder, the proprietor of the saloon, lived with his three cats and nine dogs. Jack became fairly well-known in the area as a sharp gambler, much to the dismay of his mother. Many were the times that he stared over a hand of cards at the cigar-smoke-blurred faces of men who would not hesitate to kill him if he angered them. Tucker had sometimes slipped into Scudder's Saloon in the days when Jack still lived on the ranch, marveling at his brother's bravery and cool manner while dealing cards and placing bets. He had been somewhat envious of Jack, for he was a dashing figure there at the table, but Tucker had been blessed with enough good sense to know that Jack's ways would come to no good end.

On an October evening Jack came across a piece of trouble he wasn't able to brush off with a bluff and swagger. Thurston Russell, a brute of a man, one of Danver Corrigan's chief competitors, was angered by Jack's good luck during a high-stakes game of poker. Jack had done his best to avoid bringing things to the fighting stage, but he was unsuccessful. Russell struck him, forcing him to defend himself.

For a time it was just a typical saloon brawl, onlookers told Tucker after it was over. But then the two fighters went at it in earnest, and somewhere along the line a knife was slipped into Jack's hand. No one saw just who gave it to him.

When it was over, Thurston Russell was bloody and screaming, staining the split-log floor red so fast that most who watched feared he would bleed to death. But he didn't die, though it might have been best for Jack if he had.

Thurston Russell went through life thereafter with one ear. Jack had sliced the left one off with the knife. He didn't even know himself if the act had been intentional; he had been slashing blindly, wild with rage. But when Russell recovered from his wounds, he swore that, no matter what, he would avenge himself. He wouldn't be content with merely taking an ear for an ear; he would kill Jack Corrigan, he declared.

Jack knew he meant it. So did Danver Corrigan and his wife, Bess. And rather than face the possibility of a fatal fight and more family shame, Jack moved on, heading north into the Montana Territory, working for ranches all over the eastern Montana plains, and still gambling.

Tucker had been dismayed by his brother's action for a time, for he looked on it as cowardice. Tucker was young in those days, just thirteen years old, and he found it hard to believe that anyone whom he admired as much as Jack would run from a fight. It was only a few years later that he realized the sense in what his brother had done. One moment of insanity did not justify hanging around waiting for another, possibly with worse results than a severed ear.

It was seven years now since Jack had left, and the family's communications with him had been few. They knew only that he was working on a ranch in the southeast section of the Montana Territory, near the Hanging Woman Creek, not far from the Tongue River.

"From the Crazy Woman to the Hanging Woman!" Tucker had laughed when he heard the news. But all of the family were glad Jack was so close. He was scarcely more than fifty miles to the north, and that made him seem closer than when he had been roaming up around Miles City.

But in a way he wasn't a bit closer. Even though he could be home in a two-day ride, he would not return as long as Russell held the grudge against him. It had infuriated Russell when Jack took off. When the family refused to tell him where Jack had gone, he turned a fiery red and got so bitter angry that, in Pa's words, "you could look through his ears and see his brains burnin' just like a coal stove."

But now it seemed Jack would be making the return trip in spite of Russell. That is, if Tucker could find him. When he told him Pa was dying, it would likely not be hard to convince him to come back. If only they could keep Thurston Russell away from him while he was home. . . .

Bob approached Tucker and jarred him out of his thoughts with a question: "Tuck, what did Ma say to you?"

Tucker looked shifty-eyed. "I don't know that I'm supposed to say, Bob. She pulled me to the side and talked low. If she wants you to know, she'll tell you herself."

"She's sending you after Jack, ain't she?"

Tucker said nothing, but the silence said as much as if he had nodded his head. Everyone knew Pa was dying, and it made sense that the family would want to be together one last time.

It crossed Tucker's mind as he crawled into his straw tick that night that Thurston Russell might be expecting the same thing, too. He knew Danver Corrigan was mighty sick, and he was smart enough to put two and two together.

Tucker took the best horse and rode off the next morning. His mother kissed him good-bye and cried a little in spite of herself.

"Don't cry, Ma. I'll do my best to be back with Jack in a week or so. Don't you worry."

He rode away then, for tears were gathering in his own eyes, and try as he would, he couldn't suppress the thought that he might see his pa no more.

The land to the north was beautiful, a paradise of rolling plains of wind-whipped grasses. The streams were lined with birch, and willow.

Their house had been built of straight pines. Tucker could remember how he helped Jack and his father cut the trees and drag them, using a team and chain, to the building site, where they had notched them with crude round notches and set them atop each other. Jack had wanted to take more pains with the work, but Pa said no; it was to be a temporary dwelling, and there was no point in wasting time making it too fancy. It turned out that he had been wrong about the temporary part, and Jack had been right about the notching. The temporary dwelling wound up being their permanent home, and the round notches let the logs slip and settle, making huge cracks in the mud chinking that constantly had to be repaired.

Over the years Pa turned the interior of the house into something more inviting, hewing off the inside part of the logs until the wall was something close to flat. He had installed a heavy, cast-iron stove against the back wall, setting it too close and almost burning the house down. Tucker was given the task of correcting the error by hewing out a section of that wall slightly bigger than the stove, creating a recessed area that kept the threat of fire to a minimum. It was hard work, and all because Pa had so carelessly installed the stove. Tucker loved his father, but there had been many times when the man had irritated him no end. Danver Corrigan often tended to act, then think, rather than the other way around. It was a trait the family had learned and accepted years ago.

Tucker forded the Crazy Woman and headed on toward Clear Creek. He bore to the east, moving away from the mountains and the Bozeman Trail, which cut northwest across the Little Big Horn and eventually on to Virginia City in the Montana Territory. Tucker knew the Hanging Woman cut across the border of the Wyoming and Montana territories in a north-south direction. If he could locate it, it should then only be a matter of following it and stopping at any ranch he could find and inquiring about his brother. He hoped it would be that simple.

He had a good horse and an early start. With steady plodding and few stops, he should be able to cover more than thirty miles with no problem. He would spend the night beneath the stars, then begin the actual search tomorrow.

He had eaten a substantial breakfast before setting out, and in his pack was a good supply of hard biscuit and jerked beef, along with plenty of water in a battered canteen and coffee grounds tied in a cloth sack. The small tin coffeepot dangled from the saddle.

The morning passed quickly, and long before noon his stomach was empty and grumbling about it.

He stopped five miles from Clear Creek and built a fire. Soon the small coffeepot was boiling, and Tucker laid out before him a meal of biscuit and beef, along with a small dab of honey his mother had packed for him.

He allowed himself a few extra moments of rest before continuing. He picked at his teeth with a blade of grass and thought about his father. Would he be alive when he returned with Jack? He had always taken Pa for granted, assuming he would always be around. Now that his father was on the verge of dying, he realized how precious the man was. He wasn't successful, nor perfect, but he was Pa.

Tucker stood, brushing the biscuit crumbs from his denim pants. Now wasn't the time for despairing thoughts —the sun had already crossed the crest of the sky and was heading west. It would be dark in a few hours. He saddled up quickly and started northward again at a steady lope.

He forded a creek and put several miles behind him before he stopped again. He ate a meager supper and made out his bedroll. Only after he had lain down and closed his eyes did he realize that he was lonely.

The following morning he rode until he came in sight of what he felt sure was Hanging Woman Creek. He let the horse drink, then began wandering up the west side of the water.

He came upon a small ranch after a bit more travel. It was a typical spread, consisting of a low, spread-out cabin with a dirt roof and an overhanging roof of boards over the front door. A smaller log house stood to the side of the main ranch house, and behind the whole scene was an expanse of trees partially blocking the view of the barren hills on the edge of the landscape.

Tucker took it all in, at a glance and rode slowly toward the main house. He approached close enough for anyone inside to get a look at him and did not dismount. He wore a revolver, but he kept his hands clear of it. Coming as close as he felt was reasonable, he did what folks called "hollering the house," calling out his name and asking if he might dismount. To dismount before being invited to do so would be considered rude.

A voice came back from inside the house. "Who you say you be?"

"Tucker Corrigan, from the Wyoming Territory. I'm friendly."

The front door opened, and a lanky man stepped out onto the porch. He squinted as he looked the young man over for a moment; then he set the rifle he was holding up against the wall. But he did not move away from it.

"Well, get on down, Tucker Corrigan. I got a feeling I might like to talk to you." He said it in a tone Tucker wasn't sure he liked.

Dismounting, Tucker led his horse toward the house.

Chapter 2

The man's name was Drake.

"So you're a Corrigan, are you? You know anything 'bout a man named Jack Corrigan?"

Tucker's mouth dropped open. He hadn't anticipated having his own question taken right off his tongue.

"Yes, sir—he's my brother, as a matter of fact. I come looking for him."

"Brother, huh? Well, Jack Corrigan's brother, you come a little late. He done took off."

"Took off? Was this the place he was working?"

"Yeah, he worked here. Done pretty good at the first. Then he took up with a couple of drifters named York and Dowell, and pretty soon the three of 'em took off. I knew I never should have hired them two—they had a bad look about 'em. First time I laid eyes on 'em, I says to myself, 'Billy Drake, you just send them two back the way they come,' but I was shorthanded at the time, so I thought again and took 'em on temporary. Worst mistake I could have made. They stayed on no more 'an three weeks afore they took off with your brother right along with 'em. One of the blasted fools left his ol' beat-up saddle here and took one of my best ones with him. Just took out the day after I paid 'em, they did. Took out with the best hand I'd had in years and my best saddle. If'n I see 'em again, I reckon they'll smart for it! I don't figure it was your brother what took the saddle—he didn't seem the type to steal from a man—but if'n he's willing to run with the likes of them two, maybe he ain't the honest man I thought he was."

Tucker was dismayed. He hadn't anticipated Jack's taking off for God-knows-where just at the time he needed to see him most.

"Have any idea where they might have headed?"

"Lord, boy, they didn't exactly take off wanting me to know where to find 'em. A friend of mine up about Punkin Creek said he seen three riders up in those parts a little after the time they took off from here. I reckon it was them. Said they was riding northeast, toward the Deadwood Road."

Tucker sighed. It looked as if finding Jack was going to be tougher than he had hoped. He had only a vague hint about where they might have headed, and he was not familiar with the Montana Territory. He had promised Ma he would get back with Jack within a week or so. She would be expecting him, and if he was late, she would likely worry herself sick. But coming back without Jack might put Pa in his grave all the quicker. It was a bad situation.

"Mister, I'm sure sorry about your saddle. I think I know my brother well enough to be sure it wasn't him who took it. If I run across them other two, I'll try to get your saddle back for you."

Drake threw back his head and laughed. "What do you reckon you'll do about it, boy? That saddle's gone. Your brother ain't here, and time's wasting while I sit here talking to you. Now is there anything else I can do for you?"

Tucker bristled. He had done nothing to merit the contempt evident in the rancher's voice, and certainly he could not be held responsible for the actions of his brother or his two companions.

"No, sir, I reckon you've done your best. Now, if you don't care, I'll head on so I don't waste no more of my time. You just have you a real good day."

He wheeled and headed back to his horse. As he mounted, Drake said, "If'n you run across that brother of yours, you tell him he'd best not show his face around here again, you hear? And the same goes for them two friends of his. I ain't a man who treats a thief lightly!"

Tucker rode off at a gallop, not glancing back. The rancher stood glowering until Tucker was almost out of sight, then turned back into his house, shaking his head and muttering under his breath.

Tucker was riding through a flat area of grass and a few trees. After he had put a good distance between himself and the Drake ranch, he stopped, leaning over his saddlehorn and trying to figure out what to do.

Drake had said they were heading in the direction of the Deadwood Road. If that was the case, they were probably heading for Miles City. But he could not know if they would stop there. Perhaps they would hang around town long enough to spend or gamble away their pay, or maybe they would head north or east, looking for work at one of the ranches in eastern Montana or in the Dakotas. There was no way to be sure.

Tucker did have one thing to guide him, though. He knew that Jack had one weakness—the gambling table. If he had money in his pocket, he wouldn't be likely to look for work until it ran out. Miles City would be just the place for him to gamble away his cash.

There was only one thing to do, then—head for Miles City. Tucker worried that his ma would fear for his safety if he didn't return in the time he had stated, but right now it appeared he had no choice. If his pa's last wish was to see the son who had drifted away from him, then Tucker would do his best to see that wish fulfilled.

He started riding again, grateful for the extra food his ma had packed for him.

Miles City lay at the heart of one of the nation's chief cattle-raising areas. Situated in the midst of giant plains, the city was a focal point for the life of eastern Montana.

Tucker had never been to Miles City. Once he arrived, locating Jack might be a problem. He had failed to ask Drake when Jack and his two companions had left, and that could make a big difference in whether or not he

could find them in Miles City, assuming they had gone
there at all. If Jack had a streak of luck at the gambling
table, he might hang around one area for weeks; if not,
he might leave. There were a lot of ranches in the territory, and trying to find him amidst all of them would be
nigh impossible. He hoped Jack had gone to Miles City
and stayed there.

He rode steadily, not pushing his time, for he didn't
wish to tire his mount. He thought of Pa, lying there
back on the Crazy Woman, drawing nearer the grave
with every breath. This was a hard time to be away from
him. He whispered a prayer that he could find Jack in
time to get back before Pa was dead.

Tucker bore east. He found the crisp air invigorating
and traveled for a long time before resting. He gathered
enough wood to start a small fire and brewed coffee. It
was hot and fragrant, and he made it up strong like his pa
had taught him during the many times they had worked
the roundups together. "Boil up your coffee till it can get
the rust off a nail," he had said. "In about ten minutes
after that it'll be ready to drink."

He ate a little meat and two of the biscuits. He
wanted more but didn't want to be wasteful. After waiting long enough for his meal to settle, he mounted again
and continued riding northeast.

The day passed without incident. He saw two other
ranch houses out across the plains but stopped at neither. He knew that Jack and his partners would never
stop so close to the same ranch where they had stolen a
saddle. The fact that they took property from Drake was
evidence that they had no intention of hanging around
the area. Besides, Drake had said the three riders had
been seen up around the Pumpkin Creek; he had a lot of
riding to do before he got that far.

Tucker made camp on the open plains. The wind
was cool. It rustled the grass and whistled across the
land, unimpeded by any significant obstacles. Tucker
marveled at the vastness of the land, surpassed only by

the almost ominous emptiness of the dark heavens. It was at times like these that he longed for the feeling of a roof over his head and walls surrounding him. Not because he feared the elements, but because the mysterious void of the sky would seem so deep as he lay looking up into it. There was something awesome in the nothingness of it all, almost frightening, something to make a human feel insignificant.

He shut his eyes to block out the view. Out here on the empty plains he didn't need to get himself all shivery and scared like a child.

Tucker tried to sleep, but the ground was hard and his mind was stirring. Never before had he traveled away from his home for more than a few miles unless someone was with him. Now he was striking off for a region he had never seen, with no one to guide or protect him. It was frightening in a way, yet also strangely appealing. And he knew why—for the first time in his life he felt not like a tagalong boy but like a *man*. And it was a good feeling.

Tucker rolled over and again tried to sleep, but after a few moments he realized it was no use. He stood up and stretched, determined to walk around for a bit in hopes of wearing off his excess energy. The wind struck him and he reached for his jacket, at the same time glancing carelessly toward the south.

There was a light off in the distance, a flickering light of a fire. He picked up the jacket and slipped it on, frowning. Who could it be out there? The fire was too far away from him to estimate its exact location. He had seen no one traveling the area besides himself. Unaccountably, he felt a shiver of concern.

He shrugged the feeling off. Probably the fire was in the camp of some drifter or cowboy who wanted a late-evening cup of coffee.

Tucker felt suddenly weary. He slipped off his jacket and crawled back into his blankets. He closed his eyes and listened to the wind and the sound of his horse grazing nearby, and slowly he drifted off to sleep.

When next he opened his eyes, the sun was rising and the ground was wet with dew. He rose, stretching and yawning, and looked around him. The day promised to be clear, a good one for travel. Forgotten was the awe and vague discomfort the empty land and sky had aroused in the night; now the plains were lovely, almost friendly. Building up his fire, he brewed coffee and fried a few hunks of bacon his mother had stowed deep in his sack of provisions.

He forded the creek and pushed almost due east. The best way to approach Miles City would be to follow the Deadwood Road, and he figured to reach it around Powderville.

Tucker was moving into the midst of one of the busiest cattle ranges, yet he had not yet seen a single cow. So vast was the land that animals and men were easily swallowed up in the distance or were hidden behind the low, rolling hills that spread around him. Only a few years before he would have seen buffalo, but now they were almost entirely gone, hunted to near extinction.

Tucker felt excitement begin to steal through him when he reached the Power River and the Deadwood Road. Soon he would be in Miles City, seeing things he had only heard about before, like the railroad. He was looking forward to seeing the wonder of modern transportation that ate wood and drank water while it chugged all the way from the eastern cities to the western towns, building communities and even new cities along its route. The Northern Pacific had reached Miles City a few years back. Folks were saying that the wonderful new line was changing the cattle industry remarkably. Now ranchers could drive their herds to the Miles City loading pens to be herded into big cars designed to haul stock, and the long drives to the more distant railheads were no longer necessary.

Tucker traveled as far as the light would let him before he made camp beside the road. He lay in his blankets, weary yet happy, and almost dropped off to sleep.

He recalled the fire he had seen the night before, burning toward the south. Giving a sleepy grunt, he rolled over and for a brief moment opened his eyes.

Far to the south—just how far he could not tell— the light was flickering again, just as it had the night before. Whoever had been behind him last night was still there and was apparently moving at about his rate of speed.

Chapter 3

Tucker encountered the track of the Northern Pacific just south of Miles City. Somehow the sight was a vague disappointment.

It was no more than an endless succession of ties binding together the shining rows of steel. It was hardly worth looking at. Slumping down in the saddle, he crossed the tracks and rode into the town.

Miles City was typical of many other towns in that part of the country, with wide streets and wooden buildings, many false-fronted log structures. Tucker rode directly in the middle of the street, looking from side to side at the businesses that lined it. It all looked sleepy and dull, livened only by the people moving up and down the boardwalk or walking the street.

Tucker looked at some of the saloons and wondered about Jack. It wasn't likely that he was gambling right now, for Jack had always said that it didn't seem right to cut a deck of cards until the sun was going down. But if Jack was in fact in Miles City, it seemed probable that he was registered in some boarding house or hotel. That is, unless he had chosen to make his bed on the range outside of town.

Finding Jack was the main problem, but Tucker was more concerned at the moment with buying a good meal. He was sick to his soul of jerky and dried biscuits, and the prospect of a good beefsteak with gravy and a few eggs sounded good. He eyed the stores lining the street, looking for a restaurant.

He found one and tied his horse to the hitching post

outside. Removing his hat, he entered the small log building, sniffing the tantalizing aroma of sizzling steak. He found a table in the corner and sat down.

"What'll it be?"

"Steak, two eggs fried, and about a half dozen biscuits."

The meal was delicious. Tucker topped it off with jelly on the biscuits. Sipping his coffee when the meal was through, he leaned back, feeling content and satisfied.

His leisurely and peaceful thoughts were interrupted by the memory of his father. He hoped that he would find Jack before it was too late. And too late could be very soon.

Tucker rose and paid for his meal, full but no longer happy. It was time to get down to business. Before long the gamblers would converge on the saloons to ply their art, and if Jack was in town, Tucker would find him.

The task of looking through several saloons seemed easy enough until Tucker stepped back out on the street and began counting them. Ten . . . eleven . . . twelve . . . the count continued, until he realized that on this street alone there were fourteen saloons! And there were bound to be others on the side streets. It appeared that Miles City had been founded to provide a place for drinking and carousing for the soldiers stationed at nearby Ft. Keogh.

Night fell swiftly. The last traces of light were fading in the west when Tucker stepped into the Morning Star Saloon. He looked around the interior, surprised at the elegance of the furnishings. There was velvety carpet on the floor, and fine oak and mahogany furniture. A beautifully embellished billiard table sat in prominence in the center of the room, and two men dressed in fancy black suits were engaged in a game of pool, their expensive cigars sending clouds of smoke drifting slowly up to the ceiling. Behind the bar was a large shelf backed by a mirror, and just by looking at the labels on the bottles

Tucker could tell that it was expensive liquor sold here. As the door closed behind him, several of the saloon patrons glanced his way, and something in their expressions made him conscious of his faded denims and dirty checked shirt. He glanced quickly around the room and not spying Jack, moved back outside.

He realized that he had stepped into what was surely an exclusive saloon, probably catering to rich cattlemen. A young rancher's son, still fresh into town and wet behind the ears, had no business even sticking his nose into such a plush establishment. He stepped down the boardwalk, looking for another saloon.

The next one was the antithesis of the one he had just left. The floors were covered with sawdust, and the tables were handmade and simple. Men were everywhere, rough men, most of them cowboys and some nothing in particular. The bartender was a fat, unshaven man wearing a filthy coat and grease-covered trousers on which he continually wiped his meaty hands. He had a black, drooping mustache that completely hid his mouth.

Tucker stepped into the saloon and looked around. There were a couple of card games going on, but nowhere did he see Jack. Tucker sighed but tried not to become discouraged. This was only the second place he had checked.

He was just turning to leave when a sudden disturbance erupted behind him. He wheeled about, startled, and saw immediately that trouble was coming.

Two burly men were standing and facing a third fellow, this one rather thin and hardly older than Tucker. He had been seated at one of the tables with a saloon girl on his lap, and his overturned chair betrayed the haste with which he had risen. And the liquor dripping from his shirt let Tucker know just what had happened.

One of the burly men set an empty glass down on the table and smirked at the young fellow.

"It takes a lot to get your attention, don't it, boy?

Now you just listen to me—you give your pa a message. The Circle X has been losing a lot of calves at just about the time your pa's spread has been getting more than its fair share of 'em. That don't look good to us, and it ain't gonna look good to your pa if it happens anymore. Your pa is a thief and a liar, boy, and if things don't change, he's gonna wind up stretching a rope from some cottonwood. You get your butt outta here and give him that message."

The younger man seemed to grow taller as he spat back, "If you got any messages, you deliver 'em yourself. I ain't your messenger boy, Thrasher!"

One burly man glanced at the other, a faint smile on his face. Tucker recognized in the young man the type of brashness that often got a man in trouble and sometimes got him shot.

"Son, you'd best watch your mouth. I hit you with a drink—I can hit you with a lot more," Thrasher said.

The other burly fellow spoke up. "His name's Thrasher, and he can live up to it. Now get outta here and back to your pa's ranch and deliver that message 'less you want more trouble than you can handle, boy!"

Tucker turned to leave. He didn't know how this was going to wind up, but he had no intention of hanging around to find out. He felt sympathy for the young man; he was obviously in no position to defend himself against two men twice his size, and apparently he was the son of a rancher. That fact made Tucker identify somewhat with the boy, though not enough to take a share of the punishment that was about to come to him.

Tucker was almost to the door when the crowd pressed in front of him, faces grinning, necks craning as men moved around to get a better view of the coming fight. Tucker's way out was blocked, and he stopped.

He began to shift around to the edge of the crowd, hoping to squeeze around them and out the door. Then he stopped again, but not because of the crowd. The young fellow inside didn't stand a chance, and clearly no one in the crowd was breaking his neck to help him. That rubbed Tucker the wrong way. Though he had no desire to tackle someone as big as Thrasher and his partner, he also had no desire to head out into the night knowing he had let a helpless young man get beaten half to death, or maybe even shot, without at least having tried to prevent it. What would Pa say?

Sighing and shaking his head, he turned again and looked at the spectacle on the floor. The crowd had spread itself into a circle around the sides of the room, and clearly the onlookers were prepared to enjoy a slaughter.

Blast it all—what a time to develop a code of honor! Wondering if he were a fool, Tucker began clenching and unclenching his fists, hoping that the young, victimized man would have the sense to walk out without trying to take on his two antagonists.

He didn't. With unbelievable speed the youth's fists flashed forward, crashing into the chins of Thrasher and his partner and knocking them both onto their backs on the floor. A gasp escaped from the onlookers, and whoops and shouts of delight filled the air. On the floor Thrasher gazed in shock at the ceiling, then began to roll to the side to raise himself.

He didn't make it, nor did his partner. The young lightning bolt of a fighter put a firm kick into Thrasher's chin, then wheeled around from the momentum of the kick and placed another into the temple of Thrasher's partner. Both men went down again. The young man leaped into the air, descending to dig his knee into Thrasher's big gut, his full weight smashing into the man's stomach.

Thrasher let out a combination cry and grunt that was punctuated by the sound of the young fighter's fists pounding relentlessly into his face. Thrasher's face grew bloody as the fists took their toll of his meaty features.

Tucker admired the grace and agility of the young man, realizing that the way he was handling Thrasher was gaining the respect of many others in the crowd. The catcalls and hoots were coming almost as much in favor of the young fellow as they were for Thrasher. But still, many were cheering on the burly man, cursing at him for being unable to free himself from the charge of human dynamite atop him.

Thrasher's partner was up now. His hands grasped the young man and pulled him off of the bloody and breathless fat man on the floor. The young fellow twisted loose from his grasp, turned and placed a solid blow into the man's face. Gasping, the man staggered backward, his nose shattered.

Thrasher fell like a mountain onto the young man. Thrasher's supporters sent forth a whoop of delight, urging the man to break the neck of his victim.

The young man struggled, but Thrasher's weight held him pinned to the floor. Though Thrasher held the advantage, he was still not in a good position to do much damage to the young man, for in order to keep him pinned he had to lie deadweight on top of him, making it difficult to land any solid blows.

Just as it looked like he might wriggle free, Thrasher brought his forehead down sharply into the face of the young fellow, knocking the youth's head hard against the floor. Stunned, the boy ceased struggling and Thrasher leaped up, pulling his victim to his feet. He grasped the stunned young man's arms and held him upright.

"Waynewright! Work him over!"

Thrasher's partner came forward, his face a bloody sneer. Grinning into the glazed eyes of the young man, he launched a huge fist into his gut, knocking the breath out of him and making him bend almost double, restrained only by Thrasher's grasp. Waynewright then smashed the young man in the mouth, sent another right to his gut.

His fist came back to land another blow, but absorbed in the pleasure of tormenting his victim, he failed to notice that the crowd had grown strangely silent. He swung his fist forward again.

The blow, which had been aimed for the cheekbone of the young man, never landed. A hand reached from behind Waynewright and grabbed his arm, stopping the swinging fist.

"What in the name of . . ."

Tucker smashed his fist into Waynewright's face as hard as he could, and though it felt as if he had broken his fingers in the process, he felt a strange elation when the bulking man collapsed like a puppet with severed strings. And even more enjoyable was the incredulous look on the face of Thrasher.

A whoop arose from the crowd as Tucker made for the big man, who looked completely at a loss as to how to handle his unexpected adversary while hanging on to the nearly unconscious young man he had been tormenting. Cursing, he shoved his victim forward, sending him reeling right into Tucker.

The crowd exploded. Tucker's movement into the fight was an inspiration to the fight-hungry men all around the room, and before Tucker could even shove the limp form of the young man off him, the entire saloon was rocking with a skull-busting free-for-all.

Tucker made it to his feet and lunged at Thrasher, only to be knocked aside by a flying body that some husky cowpoke had thrown across the room. Thrasher disappeared in the sea of swinging fists and bloodied faces.

Tucker was left standing in the middle of the room, not knowing how to handle what he had started, nor even sure who was fighting for him or against him. From the looks of things, he wasn't sure *anybody* knew—apparently it was a matter of smashing the most convenient face.

The young man who had been the start of it all struggled to his feet, his face bloody from a cut across his cheekbone. He stumbled toward Tucker. His hand grasped Tucker's shoulder.

Tucker jerked at his touch and started to pound his fist into the young man's face before he recognized him. The trembling fellow leaned against him, his voice cracked and low.

"Much . . . obliged to you—I . . ."

A fist struck Tucker's face and knocked him backward. He came up swinging, sending a cowboy reeling into a chair. The cowboy was on the floor nursing a broken jaw before Tucker realized that he wasn't even the fellow who had struck him.

The world became a mass of sweating, fighting muscle and flesh, and Tucker was pounded by fists like hammers. His eyes glazed and he sank into a sea of exploding, brilliant stars.

Chapter 4

Tucker was only vaguely aware of being dragged out of the saloon and helped onto a horse. Then came a ride—just how long a ride he could not tell—and he was led into some sort of dwelling and placed in a bed. His head ached horribly.

He awoke to the touch of a damp towel against his forehead. His gaze first focused on the arm that moved gently back and forth as a towel swabbed his face, then his eyes traveled up that arm to look into one of the most beautiful faces he had ever beheld.

"Hello—I thought maybe a little cold water might bring you around to us," the girl said. Her voice was clear and cheerful, and she smiled in a way that made Tucker's already limp form go limper.

"Frank told us what you did," she said. "He says you might have saved his life."

Tucker stirred and sat slightly upright, propping himself on his elbows until his senses began to return.

"Glad I could help. It wasn't a fair fight, and I thought to even the odds a little. When I jumped in, things really started humming, but after that I really can't seem to remember much . . ."

"You got busted in the head, buddy," said a male voice. Tucker looked to his right. On the other side of the bed stood the young man whom he had defended— whose name, apparently, was Frank.

Frank sat down on a stool beside the bed and extended his hand to Tucker. Still a bit groggy, Tucker reached out and shook the calloused hand, noting its strength.

"The name's Frank Bryan. And this is my sister, Charity."

"Tucker Corrigan, from south of the territory. Where am I right now?"

"I managed to get you out of that saloon without nobody noticing. Once that free-for-all started, I made it out of there all right. Things were still swinging when I got you on your horse and rode you out here to the ranch. This here's where I live, with Pa and Charity. My pa runs this spread."

Tucker looked around him. The room he was in was small, with a low ceiling. The walls were made of hewn log, smooth and almost white, for they had not yet browned with age. Tucker's bed was in the corner of the room, and across from it was a cast-iron cookstove with a flue that ran up through a hole in the roof. The walls had pegs all over them, and from those pegs hung pans and pots, two or three rifles, and some sort of crude, fuzzy painting of a cow's head, apparently hung there to add color to the room.

The ceiling was nothing but the underside of the shingled roof, with huge logs running from one end of the house to the other as support. On the side of the room was a door that opened onto a "dog trot" passageway, and beyond was another door opening into a room that was the twin of this one. Tucker recognized the common technique of making a large home from short logs by joining two small, square cabins with a common roof. Althugh he couldn't be sure from the angle at which he lay, it appeared that the Bryans had boarded up the ends of the dog trot, making the entire structure into three rooms, end on end.

Tucker glanced over at Charity Bryan, who had ceased swabbing his forehead. Her hair was a dusty brown, and her eyes were the deepest green Tucker had ever seen. Her skin was fair and unblemished. He stared at her unabashedly, until her faint smile told him his gaze bordered on rudeness. Embarrassed, he quickly turned away.

Frank Bryan was at the stove, pouring coffee into a tin mug. He walked back to Tucker's bedside and extended the mug to him.

Tucker sat completely up, feeling dizzy. It was difficult to focus his eyes. Muttering thanks, he accepted the coffee. He sipped some of the hot brew, then looked again at Frank.

"Just what was that fight all about, anyway? Why were those big devils giving you a hard time?"

Frank sat back down on the wooden stool. "Those two were Brant Thrasher and Marvin Waynewright, cowpokes for the Circle X ranch a few miles north of here. We're a small ranch, and they're a big one. We've been in operation for about two years, and they've been here for a lot longer. What it comes down to is that they're accusing my pa of rustling cattle. A lot of their pregnant cattle have been losing calves, but our herd is growing. Of course, they take it that we're stealing their newborns before they can get to 'em. Nothing we can do seems to convince 'em any different, and now they're talking about burning us out and lynching me and Pa. It's getting to be a desperate situation. I halfway thought it might not be safe to bring you out here, with folks so worked up. But there was nowhere else I could take you."

Tucker sipped his coffee, gently rubbing his aching head. "Sounds bad. But I can't see that you'll need to worry any about the likes of them two back in the saloon giving you trouble. They must be mighty big cowards to be afraid to take on a young fellow like you 'less there was two of 'em together. You gave 'em what-for for a while, Frank! I rightly admired you."

"They would have busted my head if you hadn't jumped in when you did, Tucker. I can't give you much to show my thanks, but I sure hope you know I appreciate it."

"And so do I," cut in Charity. "It's good to know there's folks like you who'll help even when they're not obliged to."

"Tucker, I'll admit I'm confused about why you did it," Frank said.

"I'm a rancher's son myself, Frank, and I guess I saw a little of me in you. My pa owns a spread down about the Crazy Woman in Wyoming. We have a small operation, too."

"That right? There's some pretty country down that way, good grazing land. What are you doing up about these parts?"

The question brought a pang to Tucker, for momentarily he had forgotten about Pa's illness and the reason he was here. He cast his gaze to the floor.

"My pa's ailing, and I come up here looking for my brother. I thought he was south of here, but folks down there told me he had moved north. Miles City seemed to be the natural place to look. I was in that saloon looking for him today."

Frank pursed his lips and slowly shook his head. "Sorry about your pa. Maybe I can help you find your brother. What's his name?"

"Jack Corrigan. I doubt you know him."

Frank shook his head. "I don't. I'll sure keep my ears open for the name, though. How long will you stay in these parts?"

"Don't know for sure. I'll hunt for Jack about a week, if it takes that, then head back whether I've found him or not. I hope I can find him. Pa was counting on seeing him before he . . . dies."

"Well, Tucker, you'll spend the night with us. It's dark already, and there's no way we're gonna have you ride back to Miles City now. Besides, I owe you for what you did."

Charity cooked up supper, and it was delicious. Thick slabs of bacon with fresh bread, molasses for sweetening. Tucker drank milk—milk that came from a can. It had always struck him as ironic that here in the heart of beef country many folks didn't bother to keep a milk cow.

He ate more than was good for him and sat back happily after the meal. Charity sat across from him, giving him a good excuse to look at her.

Frank lit up a pipe and began blowing smoke rings. The conversation dwindled. The girl became restless after a time, stood up, and walked to the window. Drawing back the curtain, she peered outside.

"It seems Pa would be back by now, Frank. I can't figure what is taking him so long."

"Don't worry, Charity. You know Pa once he gets out on the range. There's always something or other to be done. He'll be back soon enough."

But an hour passed and there was still no sign of the elder Bryan. Tucker could sense that Charity's uneasiness was beginning to be shared by her brother, who was smoking furiously, glancing toward the window every time the breeze made a random noise that might be mistaken for a hoofbeat.

Then came a noise that unmistakably *was* the sound of a hoof striking earth. Charity and Frank rose together and moved to the door. Charity threw it open, there was a moment of silence, and suddenly she said: "Frank—it *isn't* Pa . . . it's Seth Bailey!"

"Seth Bailey? What's he doing out here?"

Tucker heard the horse thunder to a stop outside, and a moment later a breathless, windblown man entered the door of the house and plopped down on a stool.

"Seth?"

"It's bad, Frank, real bad. I figured somebody had to tell you . . ."

Frank glanced at his sister, worry in his eyes. "What is it?"

"It's your pa, Frank. They done got him locked up in the jail—charged him with rustling."

Frank collapsed into a chair. Charity went pale.

"When, Seth?"

"Not long after sundown. Don't know all the details, but I seen the sheriff taking him into the jailhouse myself. And Dan Granger was with him."

Frank bent forward, resting his face in his hands. Charity moved over behind him, biting her lower lip to keep from crying, and placed her hand on her brother's shoulder.

Frank rose up again after a moment and looked seriously at Seth Bailey. "I gotta go into town," he said. "I gotta see my pa."

"I figured you would, Frank. Be careful."

Tucker stood. "Frank, I'm going with you."

The young man turned and looked at Tucker. "Tucker, there's no reason for you . . ." He paused, then grinned in a rather sad way. "Thanks, Tucker. I 'preciate it."

The pair saddled up and headed for Miles City. For quite some time they said nothing to each other, then Tucker pulled up close beside Frank.

"Who is this Dan Granger?"

"Owner of the Circle X, and a real troublemaker. He's been after Pa for months now."

"And who is Seth Bailey? Can you trust him?"

"Sure. Seth has been a family friend for a long time. He's always done his best to stick up for Pa. He lives alone in a shack a couple of miles from our spread. Raises his food, works a few of the roundups when the mood strikes him. He's lazy, but a good man."

"Do you think it was wise to leave him alone with Charity?"

"Sure—better than having her there alone. Don't worry, Tucker. He's trustworthy."

Tucker hoped so. He was surprised at how protective he felt toward a girl he had just met and had hardly spoken to.

They reached Miles City and rode straight for the

jailhouse. It had a foreboding look, and Tucker wondered just what Frank planned to do once he got in there. Tying his horse to the front hitching rail, Tucker followed the young rancher's son onto the board porch of the jailhouse.

Frank didn't hesitate at the door, nor did he knock. He flung the door open and barged inside, walking straight to the desk and the startled lawman behind it. He slapped his palms down onto the desktop and leaned forward until his face was no more than a foot away from the sheriff's.

"My name's Frank Bryan. You got my pa locked up for rustling, and I'm here to tell you he ain't done it. You can turn him loose."

The sheriff rose. Tucker was amazed at how tall he was. As he looked down into Frank's face, he made the young man look puny by comparison. But Frank returned his gaze fearlessly.

"Look, boy, if you're Duke Bryan's son, you'd best know that I got you pa dead to rights. Dan Granger swore, along with two others, that he caught your pa rustling earlier this evening. I had no choice but to lock him up. And until we find out more about this, I got no plans to let him loose."

Frank looked a bit chastened, for obviously there was nothing he could do. He stared into the sheriff's face for a moment, then asked in a slightly less forceful voice: "Could I see him?"

The sheriff sighed. He led the two young men back to the cell area, throwing open the heavy door that separated it from the front office. A scent of unwashed bodies assaulted Tucker's nose.

The jail was full tonight, mostly with drunks and brawlers. Blank faces stared at the three men as they moved back farther into the cellblock. There were two men in each cell; in some there were three.

Frank moved to the cell where a bearded man sat in dejection on a bed chained to the wall. When he saw

Frank, the man brightened, then looked all the more despondent.

"They got me up a creek this time, boy. They surely do."

A slender man sharing the same cell turned to look at the trio. As he laid eyes on Tucker, his mouth fell open in shock. Tucker's did the same.

"Jack? Is it you? Jack!"

Chapter 5

Charity Bryan poured Seth Bailey a cup of coffee, which he accepted with thanks. He watched the young lady walking nervously around the room.

She turned to him and asked pleadingly, "Seth, why is there so much stir over rustling right now? Why is Granger so determined to hurt my pa?"

"I can't answer the second part of that question, Charity, 'cause I don't know what Granger has against your pa in particular. But the reason there's so much trouble over rustling is that so much of it is going on. More and more cattle are disappearing, and when a small rancher like your pa starts doing well at about the time the big ranchers are losing out, it's only natural they would get suspicious. But you ought to not feel real bad about this—it could have been a sight worse."

"Worse? What could be worse than having my pa in jail for rustling?"

"Havin' him strung up, that's what! Granger figures your pa is a rustler, and from his point of view he was doing him a mercy by taking him to the jail instead of hanging him on the spot. That's what a lot of cattlemen are doing to the rustlers lately, whether they have been convicted or not. Some have even took away prisoners from the law and . . ."

He stopped, sorry he had mentioned that lynchings had been occurring under the very nose of the law; with Duke Bryan locked up, such talk was hardly comforting to his daughter.

"Seth, do you think . . ."

"No, Charity. I'd say your pa is safe right now. They ain't gonna bust right in that jail to get him. Don't you worry."

He took a sip from his cup and hoped he was right. He wasn't nearly as confident about it as he pretended. In eastern Montana and western Dakota, ranchers were beginning to talk to each other about the rise in rustling. Many were recommending a range war—a unified effort to wipe out the thieves who took advantage of the ranchers' inability to watch their stock out on the open range. Other ranchers were trying to approach the situation with moderation, favoring moves such as the hiring of range detectives and extra hands to keep watch over their stock, but increasingly their voices were being drowned out with louder, more angry ones. Seth was a good friend of Duke Bryan, but he was realistic enough to know that Granger was a strong enough man to have Bryan strung up to a cottonwood at a moment's notice. So far, he was being merciful.

Charity could tell from the nervous way Seth was sipping his coffee that things were not as bright as he was making them out. He was correct in saying that it was lucky Pa was just locked up instead of dead, but she had lived the life of a rancher's daughter long enough to know that no prison could keep determined men from taking out their wrath on a prisoner. And Dan Granger was a man with a remarkable ability to stir up hatred when he wanted to. Dan Granger got what he wanted, when he wanted it, or others paid the price.

What Granger's motive was for his continued actions against her father baffled her. If only Ma were still living—she could have talked to her about it. Ma had always understood problems like that, it seemed. She had been a woman with a keen insight into the human heart and mind.

Charity walked over to the window and stared out into the darkness. The night was silent but for the wind that whistled around the eaves of the house, the moan of it sad and lonesome. She wondered how Pa was, locked up there in the jailhouse, and if Frank and Tucker had managed to talk to him, maybe even get him freed.

She longed to hear the sound of hoofbeats coming over the rise, yet she also dreaded it. The sound of those hooves could herald either the return of Pa, or perhaps merely more bad news. It was hard to believe that such a short time ago things had been so good, the family all together, the future promising.

"Maybe you should sit down, get a little rest," Seth suggested. "I'll tell you what—I'll go on into the other room if you would like to go to bed. It's getting late, and you might need to catch a little sleep. I'm heading outside for a smoke and some fresh air, but I'll be close by. If you need anything, just holler."

Charity smiled at the ragged man. Seth had proven himself a good friend many times over, and it comforted her to have him near. Seth was a good-hearted soul, as homely as they come, and she felt toward him much as she would toward some sort of ugly, lovable old billy goat. She felt secure with him, too, for she knew he had a reputation as a crack shot. She had seen him only a few times without his Colt strapped to his hips.

"Thank you, Seth. I don't think I'll be able to sleep until Frank gets back, but it might feel good to lie down anyway. If you hear them coming, let me know."

"Sure will, Charity."

Seth stepped outside, leaving Charity alone. She walked over to the stove and placed a few extra pieces of wood inside, making the blaze flare to new brightness. She swung the metal door closed and walked over to her bed.

She didn't undress, for she wanted to be able to rise at a moment's notice when Frank and Tucker returned. She had no intention of going to sleep, but when she laid her head on the feather-stuffed pillow, she became drowsy and soon was dozing.

Outside, Seth drew on his pipe, watching the burning tobacco glow red and bright with every puff. He was deep in thought, and his eyes were continually drawn to the dark slope over which Frank and his young partner would come riding when they returned. He hoped Duke would be with them but knew it was unlikely.

And he knew that he was the only man who understood Granger's true motives. He longed to tell Charity the truth, but that was impossible. Still, it was so hard to continue in a lie, especially at a time like this. But it really wasn't his choice. He had made a promise, one he had to keep.

He leaned up against the wall. He liked the feel of the sturdy logs; it made him a bit sad, though, for it revived an old dream that long ago had perished. He had once dared to hope that one day he would own a ranch of his own, somewhere here on the plains, and maybe he would even have had a fine wife and a daughter like Charity or a son like Frank. That was a dream from years ago, though. At moments like this, it would revive itself for a moment, but something would always happen to pull Seth into the more mundane world of reality.

And in this case that something was a stirring in a grove of trees just a few yards across from the cabin and slightly toward the west. Seth tensed and listened closely; he didn't like what he had heard, for the sound had an element of stealth in it. Slowly his hand crept toward his gun butt.

He stared into the dark growth of trees and spoke in a voice loud enough to carry across the distance while not disturbing Charity inside the house.

"Who is it? I hear you . . . and I'll shoot if you don't show yourself!"

For a moment there was no sound, but then came the faint but easily discernible snapping of a twig beneath a foot, then a clicking noise that could only be one thing.

Seth's pistol whipped from his holster and began spitting red flame into the night, bullets ripping through leafy branches and slapping into tree trunks with a dead, plunking sound.

Then the fire was answered with echoing blasts from the grove, just as Seth was overcome by panic, blindly emptying the chamber of his Colt at a target he could not see.

The sheriff looked at Tucker suspiciously. "You know this fellow?" he asked, gesturing toward Jack Corrigan, who stood staring at Tucker as if he were an apparition.

"Yes, sir. He's my brother."

"Well, you know your brother's a rustler, do you? Maybe you do . . . maybe you know a lot about it!"

Tucker could read the sheriff's thoughts, and it angered him. But it scared him to think that Jack was being held on so serious a charge.

"Tucker—what are you doing here?" Jack asked. "How did you get here?"

"I was about to ask *you* that!" exclaimed Tucker. "What's this about you rustling cattle?"

"It's a stinking lie, that's what it is! A bunch of circumstances that made me look bad. I've never rustled a cow in my life and don't plan to start. But it ain't no use trying to tell that fool sheriff that!"

The sheriff stared coldly at Jack. "You keep up that talk, and I'll cut off your visiting privileges with your brother here. You were caught riding with known rustlers."

Jack's eyes narrowed. He looked squarely into the face of the tall sheriff. "I told you how I met them. I knew absolutely nothing about anything they might have done before, and I sure had nothing to do with it myself. You got no reason to hold me here."

The sheriff simply stared back at him, obviously unmoved. Frank Bryan and his father stood regarding the situation, apparently confused. Duke Bryan had no idea who Tucker was. Frank quietly gave a brief account of how he had met Tucker and how Granger's toughs had tried to beat him senseless in the saloon.

Jack and Tucker fell into a deep conversation, trying in a few moments' time to fill in the events of seven years. Tucker told Jack of their father's illness, and Jack was visibly shaken.

"I knew something like that would happen sooner or later. I never should have left. I should have had it out with Thurston Russell."

Tucker shook his head. "I don't think it matters now. The main thing we gotta do is get you outta here so you can see Pa. It's important to him."

The sheriff was lighting a pipe, slowly drawing on the flame until the tobacco was glowing evenly. He shifted the pipe stem to one side of his mouth and dropped the match to the brick floor.

"Forget it, boy. He ain't going nowhere until we determine the truth about that rustling charge."

Duke Bryan, a lean, tanned man with a stubbly beard and small eyes, laughed contemptuously. "In this country what Granger says will go, and if he so much as hints that somebody is rustling cattle, there ain't nothing to look forward to except a prison rock pile or a noose."

The sheriff looked sharply at Bryan. "Shut up, you. Nobody will hang or go to prison without a trial. Granger has no control over that."

"Granger pulls the strings here, and you know it. You jump when he hollers and dance when he whistles just like everybody else in this territory. And if he came knocking on your door tonight politely asking to lynch every man in this jail, you'd step aside and let him do it," the rancher snapped. "I was locked up here without a trace of evidence against me, just because Granger claimed I was rustling. You're a puppet, Sheriff."

Tucker could feel the sting of contempt in Duke Bryan's voice. He was clearly a man who had been pushed to his limit, harassed until he could stand it no longer.

Duke Bryan turned to Frank. "Where is Charity? Is she alone?"

"Seth Bailey is with her, back at the ranch. She'll be all right."

"I hope so. But I'm worried about Granger. His men took me right on the range. Almost like Granger had decided on the spur of the moment to get me out of the way. I'm worried about what he might do back home."

"I thought about that, too, Pa. But there wasn't much I could do. That's why I came here, hoping that some way I could get you out."

Duke Bryan laughed. "And how did you plan to do that? Bust the sheriff in the head?"

Frank caught the slightly different tone in his father's voice. The young man looked into Duke's eyes and did not miss the covert command in them. He smiled faintly, and his father did the same.

The sheriff was leaning against a brick column, still puffing on his pipe and listening to the talk with a quiet, arrogant air. He did not catch the hidden order Duke Bryan had directed at his son.

So he was not prepared when the young man wheeled suddenly, a hard fist swinging up from his waist to catch him full in the chin. The lawman bit the stem of his pipe in half as the force of the blow lifted him two inches off the floor. He slammed back against the wall, collapsing to his rump with hissing breath escaping his lips.

For a moment there was only silence within the jail, Then the prison became a virtual madhouse, with prisoners roaring out in delight at what Frank had done, demanding immediate freedom. Two men in the adjoining cell began shouting, extending their arms through the bars in supplication to Frank to let them go. Tucker took them to be the pair Jack had taken up with, the same ones who had stolen the saddle from the Drake ranch on the Hanging Woman Creek.

"Frank, do you think you should have done that?" asked Tucker, awed. "When he comes to . . ."

"When he comes to we'll be long gone," responded Frank, now kneeling beside the unconscious lawman and removing the ring of keys from his belt. "We had no choice—I have to get Pa out of here, and there's no way you can get your brother back to your ranch unless you break him loose. Is this the key, Pa?"

"I think so . . . hurry up! There's a deputy here somewhere."

The cell door swung open, and Duke Bryan exited the cell, Jack right after him, looking a bit dazed at his unexpected freedom. Duke bent and took the pistol from the sheriff's gun belt.

"Our stuff is all locked up in the safe outside," he said. "We'll have to make do with what we can find as far as weapons and ammunition."

Tucker caught Frank's arm. "Frank—do you realize what this means? We're putting ourselves on the run from the law. Is it worth it?"

"It's the only choice we have! I won't stand back and see my pa get jailed and maybe lynched. Granger has lynched men before, and I don't doubt he would do it again. He would hang your brother just as quick, too. Now shut up and get moving!"

Tucker obeyed, heading into the jail office. Duke Bryan had already rounded up several rifles and a good supply of ammunition.

"We've got two horses outside—we'll have to steal a couple of others," said Frank. "There should be plenty in front of the saloon."

Tucker stopped short. "Listen, Frank—we're in trouble enough as it is, and I won't be a party to horse stealing! This has gone far enough."

"The only choice you have is to get away fom here any way you can, or march your brother back into that cell! If you leave, you're already in truble with the law, whether you steal a horse or not. We're not playing games, Tucker—are you with us or not?"

Tucker glanced at his brother, and a silent communication passed between them. He said, "We're with you."

Duke Bryan shoved open the door and peered out cautiously into the night before stepping onto the porch. The street wasn't deserted, but no one seemed to be paying attention to them. Tucker's horse was still there, tied to the hitching post beside Frank's.

"Pa, you take my horse. I'll get one in front of the saloon over here. It's more important that you get away than it is that I do."

"I'm waiting on you, Son. We'll all leave together."

"I'll go with you, Frank," Jack said.

Tucker and Duke mounted horses, rifles across their laps. Jack and Frank started walking nonchalantly toward the nearest saloon. There were a half dozen horses tied to the rail in front of it, whose owers, they hoped, were too busy bending their elbows to take notice of what was about to happen outside.

Jack reached the nearest horse. He loosened the ties from the rail and pulled himself into the saddle as Frank did the same with the chestnut tied beside Jack's horse.

Clicking his tongue and moving back from the rail, Jack turned the horse and headed down the street toward the jail. Frank did the same, sending a hurried look toward the saloon door.

A figure appeared there, a staggering man, big and husky and very drunk. Against the bright background of the well-lighted saloon, he was to Frank's eyes a silhouetted form, his features invisible as he pushed the door farther ajar and gazed for a moment at the young man riding his horse toward the edge of town.

"My horse! He's stole my horse!"

All four of the men in front of the jail nudged their heels into the flanks of their horses, urging the animals into a run. The man in the saloon door staggered forward, arms waving, shouting after the rapidly fleeing riders.

Others followed him from the door then, one of

them finding that his horse also was stolen. But the four riders had disappeared into the darkness, and most of the men reentered the saloon.

The big drunken man and the other victim of Frank and Jack's thievery did their best to convince someone, anyone, to go after the vanished riders, but their pleas were unheeded.

It was at that moment that the sheriff appeared on the porch of the jail, rubbing his head with one hand and his jaw with the other. Dazed, straining to focus his eyes, he stared into the darkness, aware that his prisoners would not easily be found.

The two men from the saloon came up to him on the porch, too angry about the theft of their horses to notice the sheriff's condition. The big drunken one leaned right into the lawman's face and demanded that he ride after the thieves.

The sheriff pushed him aside, ignoring him. "Shut up—I gotta go talk to Dan Granger!"

He stepped off the porch and headed for the livery, weaving and staggering. The two men on the jailhouse porch stared after him stupidly, shrugged, and headed back to the saloon.

Chapter 6

The men rode hard for a time, at last stopping for a brief rest about two miles out of town. There had been no sign of pursuit, but still the darkness seemed pregnant with danger and all of the riders were tense.

Frank reined his horse in beside his father's. "Where can we go, Pa? They'll come looking at the ranch."

"I know, Frank. But Charity's there. We gotta go back and see that she's all right. I'm afraid of what might happen if some of Granger's men get there before we do."

"What about Tucker and his brother here? They got no cause to get involved any further."

Tucker turned to gaze at his brother, waiting for a response. He sensed that the logical thing to do was to politely thank Frank and his father for their help in freeing Jack, but something in him was resisting that notion. He found himself hoping that Jack would desire to throw in with the rancher and his son and help them fight their way out of their desperate situation.

Jack looked at Tucker, then at the others. "Men, I don't know just what all of this is about, but I'm obliged to you for my freedom. And if you're in some sort of trouble, I feel inclined to help get you out of it. I don't know a lot about this Granger fellow, but I heard his name thrown around when that lawman locked me up. I think it was him that had me arrested. If Tucker is willing, I'm for seeing this through, as long as we can."

Tucker was willing. Frank broke into a grin, and Duke leaned over to pat Tucker on the shoulder.

"I don't really know you, young fellow, but I'm thankful you're along. And you, too, Jack. I don't know if you're a rustler or not, but right now I don't really care."

"I ain't a rustler, though I do consider myself somewhat of a fool, for I been riding with a couple of them the last few weeks. That's the only reason I didn't ask you to let 'em out when you freed me—they got me into some fine messes already, and I'm happy to take my leave of them."

"Men, I don't want to break up a good conversation, but we'd best be riding," said Frank. "Charity's waiting, and that sheriff might have a posse on our tail before long."

The men set out again, riding steadily, though not as hard as before. Tucker thought over what Frank had said. It seemed likely that the sheriff would get a posse together to pursue them. It seemed equally likely that the posse would catch up with them, probably at the ranch. And then . . . He shuddered to think about it.

Tucker had never been involved in any significant battle in his life, and he had never figured he would be. Most of the time he didn't carry any weapon, except when he was out on the range, and though he was a good shot, he had never enjoyed training his sights on any living thing, whether a jackrabbit or a lame horse. And the idea of lining up a gun on a man and pulling the trigger . . . that was hard to think about.

Tucker didn't have any idea how late it was, though he knew it was well past midnight. Charity would probably be upset by now, worrying all this time about her pa and brother. For a moment he caught himself wondering if she had been worrying about him, too, but he chided himself for such a fool notion.

He felt a great surge of relief to see the ranch house still standing as they rode up within sight of it. From the way Duke had been talking, he had feared that the ranch might have been burned down long before they arrived.

The men rode to the front of the house and dis-

mounted. It wasn't until then that Tucker sensed that
something was wrong. Just what it was he couldn't say,
but apparently the same sense had gripped Duke and
Frank, for both looked at each other, frowning.

Tucker realized then that Charity had not come out
to greet them. He gripped his rifle and looked to the
others, not sure what to do.

Duke and Frank eased toward the door, holding
their rifles. It was a tense situation, for while they did
not want to walk into some sort of trap, at the same time
they didn't want to startle Charity. Maybe she had dozed
off during the long period of waiting. Having four armed
men burst through the door would be a shock to her.

Tucker and Jack stood back near the horses while
Frank and his father approached the ranch house. Frank
crept to the window and peeped over the sill, trying to
see through an opening in the curtains. It was no use;
they were closed tightly.

Frank crept over to where his father crouched beside the door. "Where's Seth Bailey? If he was still here,
I think he would have been on the lookout for us."

"I know. That worries me."

Duke turned to Tucker and Jack, motioning for
them to stay where they were. Then he and his son took
a deep breath, readied their rifles, and reached for the
latchstring.

The door flew open, and a tormented cry escaped
from the interior of the house, followed almost immediately by a gunshot. Tucker ducked where he stood near
the horses, hearing the lead wing away over his head and
into the night.

Duke and Frank leaped into the doorway, aiming
their rifles at the crouching figure cowering beside the
cookstove on the opposite side of the room.

It was Charity, pale, frightened, and gripping a rifle. She dropped her weapon and ran into the arms of
her father. Tucker and Jack, still uncertain about what

was happening inside the house, moved carefully to the door and looked in before entering.

Frank and his father were too involved with a rather emotional reunion with Charity to notice what Tucker saw immediately when he entered the room.

Seth Bailey lay stretched out on the bed, his face white and his mouth open, his eyes staring. His shirt was a bloody, bullet-pocked rag. At first glance Tucker could tell he was dead.

Charity was crying, her arms around Frank's neck, when Duke Bryan turned to see Tucker staring at the bed. Following the young man's gaze, he took in the dead form of his old friend, and his face seemed to age ten years.

"Seth . . ."

He walked toward the bed. Frank looked up also and noticed Seth's body. His breath drew in with a hiss. Without realizing it, he gripped Charity's arms with such a force that she had to pull away.

Duke turned toward his daughter. "Charity, what happened?"

The girl wrapped her arms around herself as if she were cold. "I can't tell you exactly what happened, Pa. I was inside, getting ready to lie down and rest until you and Frank got back, and there was shooting all at once. It was over almost as soon as it started. I could hear Seth crying out for help; he sounded like he was hurt bad, and there were men moving around in the trees outside, just up the slope.

"I got the rifle and went to the window. I could see Seth on the ground. There were several wounds in his chest. Then two men started moving toward him up in the darkness, and I fired at them. I didn't really aim, I don't think—I just pointed the gun in their direction and fired.

"They took off running, but I don't think I hit them. And I didn't recognize them—I don't think they were Granger's men."

Duke frowned. "Then why were they there? And why would they shoot at Seth and come toward the house?"

"I don't know, Pa. Maybe they *were* Granger's men. But I've seen most of his riders at one time or another, and I had never seen these. One of them was fat, with a beard. It was dark, but I think the hair was red. The other man was fat, too, with dark hair and a mustache. When I started shooting, they didn't hang around long."

Tucker stepped forward. "You say one had a red beard?"

"Yes."

"Did you notice anything else?"

"No . . . why? Do you think you might know who it is?"

Jack spoke then, for the first time since they had come in. "My name is Jack Corrigan, ma'am. I'm Tucker's brother. I think I might know who it was. It might be a man who is out to get me, a man named Thurston Russell. Tucker came here from the Wyoming Territory because our pa is dying. Russell might have followed him, figuring Tucker would lead him to me."

Jack turned away. Tucker could sense what his brother was thinking. He was wondering if it was because of him that a man was dead, a man he didn't even know. If that *was* Thurston Russell haunting the dark plains outside, then only because of Jack was he in the area.

Frank put his arm around his sister's waist. "Did Seth talk to you?"

Charity pulled away from her brother quickly, looking suddenly evasive. She spoke quickly. "No. He said nothing. Nothing at all." She moved over to the window and looked outside, as if trying to avoid looking at the others. Frank and Duke glanced at each other but said nothing.

Duke walked to the door and opened it, looking at the sky. "It won't be long till morning. I sure as the dickens ain't going to try to sleep. I'm way too tensed up, and it could be that Granger might send some of his men in here after us."

Frank said, "The sheriff will have a posse here before long."

Duke sat down on a bench up against the front wall. "I don't know what to do, Frank. I won't lie to you. If we fight it out, there's a good chance we'll be killed. They won't take us back to the prison. But on the other hand, if we run out, Granger's won. He wants the small ranchers out of here so the range can belong to him. If we give in, it'll make it bad for the others." Duke put his elbows on his knees and dropped his chin into his cupped palms.

Frank turned again to Tucker and Jack. "Pa's right. We can't ask you to risk your lives for us, no matter what we said before. If you want to leave, now's the time. Granger might get here before dawn."

Tucker was scared, and Frank knew it. And Jack hardly knew what was going on, despite the brief explanations. He had been thrown into the middle of the situation through no fault of his own, and Tucker wouldn't blame him if he wanted to move on. Back on the trail he had said he would stay. Turning to his brother, Tucker asked him if he still felt the same way.

Jack's response was firm and clear. "If Thurston Russell did this to this man," he said, gesturing toward Seth Bailey's body, "then I ought to stay around here and do something about it. We said we would stick it out, and I ain't one to change my mind. I got even more reason now that Thurston Russell might be involved."

Duke stood. "All right then. There's something I want you to do for me, Tucker. There might be a gunfight here soon. I don't want Charity around when it happens. I want you to pack up supplies for a good while, then ride with Charity out to an old line-camp cabin ten miles south of here. Stock her up good, get her moved in, then stay there until one of us comes out to tell you it's over.

I'm putting my daughter's safety—and her honor—in your hands. Take good care of her."

Tucker nodded. "Yes, sir."

"Thank you, boy. Jack, if you're willing, stay on here with me and Frank. I might be putting your neck in a noose, but if you really want to stick it out like you said . . ."

"I do. I'll stay as long as need be."

"Thank you. And you, too, Tucker. I hope I can pay you back someday."

Charity cut in. "I'll start gathering supplies, Pa. It won't be long till first light." She began bustling about the room, gathering food and clothing and stuffing them into a burlap bag. She put on a valiant show for a few minutes, then the dread overwhelmed her and she ran to her father, collapsed into his arms, and wept.

Chapter 7

Tucker and Charity rode away from the ranch shortly before dawn, moving swiftly, each carrying a rifle. Tucker had a pistol strapped to his waist as well. Duke Bryan had given it to him.

Tucker tried to concentrate on the trail ahead, but he felt as if eyes were watching him all around, as if the gradually lightening plains were filled with danger. He kept Charity close as they traveled.

In a way it was Charity who led, for Tucker knew nothing of the exact whereabouts of the old line camp. But Charity knew the plains well and guided her horse swiftly and surely toward the south, moving with the assurance of a seasoned rider. Tucker admired her grace and skill in the saddle, knowing that if worse came to worse, she could probably evade any pursuers even without his help.

The dawn broke golden over the eastern horizon, its rays catching the shimmering of sweat on the flanks of the horses and the shining of Charity's hair as it whipped behind her in the morning wind.

Tucker occasionally looked behind to see if they were being pursued, but there was never anything except the eternal rolling of the prairie and an occasional tree or outcrop of rock. That much was good.

Of course, there was still Thurston Russell to think about. Everybody back on the Crazy Woman knew Danver Corrigan was ailing, and it didn't take much to figure out he would want to have his family reunited before the end came. Maybe Russell had anticipated what would happen and had followed Tucker. Tucker thought about the distant fire he had seen as he traveled northward. Could it have been the campfire of Thurston Russell? It made sense.

Tucker and Charity made good time. When the sun was well above the line of the horizon and its rays were hot against their faces, Charity pulled her horse to a stop.

"The line camp is over there," she said, pointing to a slope that was dotted with scrubby trees and brush. "That stream runs within ten feet of it."

"Do you think anybody will be there?"

"It could be. I suppose we should check it out before we ride in."

Charity clicked her tongue, and her horse headed for the slope. The girl had the confidence of any cowpoke in the saddle. She had quiet authority over her mount that came only after years of experience in riding. The girl had worked alongside her father and brother in roundups during the lean years when it was hard to hire help. She knew as much about the ranching business as many of the cattle tycoons who puffed big cigars in the stockgrowers' meetings in Miles City.

When Tucker and Charity reached the brink of the slope, they dismounted and tied their horses inside a clump of low brush. Then they carefully moved forward, crouching to keep out of sight in case there was someone in the line camp.

It was built right into the side of a hill. The rear wall of the little structure was nothing more than the rock and dirt of the hill itself.

"Looks deserted enough," whispered Tucker.

"It probably is," Charity said. "But let's be sure. Toss a stone against that door there."

Tucker did as the girl instructed, lobbing a fairly heavy chunk of sandstone into the rough timber of the door. It made a hollow, clunking sound.

They waited for a full minute. There was no movement or noise. They rose and carefully entered the cabin.

The cabin was a mess, dusty and strewn with old cans, ragged scraps of clothing, and empty bottles. Apparently it hadn't been used as a line camp for quite some time, though drifters had apparently made it a temporary quarters. And from the general smell of the place, it seemed a few animals had used it as a den.

Charity had said little while they were traveling, which Tucker had attributed to worry over her family. He was worried, too, fearing for Jack's welfare. Yet he admired his brother for his willingness to risk his very life to help a family he hardly knew. Jack had his bad habits and a powerful temper, but there was a lot to be said for his bravery and unselfishness.

As the day passed, Charity began to talk more, losing her worries somewhat in the bustle of cleaning up the cabin. Tucker helped her, carrying out trash, sweeping out the old cans and bottles, brushing away cobwebs and dust. He wondered if Charity was uncomfortable in his presence. She didn't seem to be. Everything she said indicated she was glad he was around.

Tucker found her presence enjoyable, but he felt distracted. He wondered what was going on back at the Bryan ranch. If there was to be a battle, he figured it had probably taken place by now. Jack, Frank, Duke . . . they might all be dead already. He wondered if Charity realized that.

She did. And it was primarily because of that realization that she tried to lose herself in her work. It was troubling to be miles away, unable to help.

But what could she do? Pa would never let her take part in the battle. There would be nothing at all she could do.

Unless . . .

One possibility—a slim chance, a daring one, but perhaps one that would help. But could she do it? Failure might only make things worse.

She certainly couldn't do what she was thinking about with Tucker nearby. As long as he was around, she would be tied to this spot. If only there was some way to convince him to return to the ranch, leaving her alone to carry out her scheme. . . .

Tucker brought in a rabbit for their supper about an hour before dusk. Charity had found an old black pot tucked away in the corner of the cabin, and now that it had been cleaned and scoured and a fire had been built in the rough stone fireplace, she was ready to cook up a stew. With some of the potatoes and carrots she had brought along, and topped off with some fresh fire-baked bread, it would be a fine meal.

Tucker sat and watched Charity stirring the stew, feeling a bit out of place. All it took was a glance for her to turn him into a shy, stuttering boy.

The stew was first-rate. Tucker downed two bowls of it. He sat sipping his coffee when the meal was over, eating a slab of the fresh bread, topped by apple jelly they had brought along for sweetening.

Charity grew quiet. Tucker knew what she was thinking about. Conversation dwindled, and for several long minutes they sat in silence, contemplating their own thoughts.

"Tucker?"

"Yes, Charity?"

"What do you think has happened at the ranch?"

"I don't know, Charity. I wish I did."

"Me, too."

"Don't you worry—there wasn't a man there who didn't know how to take care of himself." He winced inwardly when he realized he had inadvertently spoken in the past tense, and he hoped Charity hadn't noticed.

"When do you think we'll find out?"

"Soon. They said they would come and tell us when it's safe to go back."

Charity stood and walked over to the fire. "That was before dawn this morning. If there was a fight, it would have taken place already. But still there's been no word. I'm afraid they might be dead."

Tucker looked down at the dirt floor. He could say nothing to ease her worries, for he was thinking the same thing. If the defenders had successfully held off Granger's men and avoided arrest or lynching, then they would have been able to reach this line camp long ago.

"Tucker . . . I don't think I can stand it any longer. I want you to take me back and see what happened."

Tucker frowned. "You know your pa gave me strict orders to stay here with you until we got word to leave."

"Then go alone and bring word back to me. I'll be all right here alone." Charity held her breath; she had made the first request hoping he would turn it down, a sort of bluff to keep him from realizing that what she truly wanted was the second option she had presented.

"I don't know, Charity . . . I made a firm promise to your pa. He wouldn't be pleased if I didn't keep it. Besides, I can't leave you here by yourself. There ain't no telling who might show up. It's obvious drifters have used this place before."

"I can take care of myself. But Pa and Frank, not to mention your brother, might be in sore shape right now. They might need you. It could be that they're back in that jail again, just waiting for someone to haul them out and lynch them. Maybe they can't come out here— maybe they're hoping you'll come back."

Tucker felt his will breaking. Against his better judgment, he relented. "All right, Charity—I'll go. But promise me one thing—you'll not open this door to anybody except me or one of the others from the ranch."

She agreed readily. Tucker began making his preparations, still believing it was all a mistake. But he had given his promise to her. He tried not to think about the fact that he was already breaking the promise he had made to Duke Bryan.

But even as Tucker threw the saddle on the horse and pulled tight the girth, he knew that his going was not entirely motivated by Charity's request. Deep inside he, too, was worried about the lack of word from the ranch. Something must have happened there to keep them from sending word as they had promised.

Charity watched him leave, moving north in the darkness, and suddenly she felt alone and afraid. The line camp cabin became frightening, dark and ominous, and the empty plains seemed to hold invisible phantoms. But no matter. She would not long remain here. With Tucker gone, there was no one to keep her from fulfilling her mission. It wasn't something she looked forward to, but it was something she had to do. If only she wouldn't be too late . . . if only the battle at the ranch had somehow been put off. . . .

She moved back toward the cabin. There was not a moment to lose. She would give Tucker just enough time to get a good distance ahead of her, then she would follow.

But she would not go to the ranch. She wouldn't have time, as much as she would like to do it. She had to go to the only place where she might be able to stop with words what otherwise might explode into violence, if it hadn't already. She would go armed with information Seth Bailey had gasped out to her the night before, a secret he had kept for years.

She would go to Dan Granger.

Chapter 8

Duke Bryan's heart had been heavy when he watched his daughter ride away beside Tucker Corrigan. Frank stood beside him. "Don't you worry, Pa. They'll be back safe and sound."

Duke nodded. "I know. And what will they find when they get here?"

Inside the log ranch house, Jack was having his own worries. Partly he felt like a fool for being here, risking his neck against heaven knows what danger, and all for folks he hardly knew. But he had been reared with a strong sense of duty, and there was no way he could back out.

Especially if his suspicions about Thurston Russell proved true. Many had been the time when he had thought about Russell over the past years, wondering if the old wound was still festering, pondering the incredible strength of the thing called hate. Russell was a man with a reputation for cruelty, certainly not the kind to forget old grievances.

Outside, the darkness was thick, concealing the surrounding plains. Would Tucker be able to safely guide Charity through the night to the line camp Duke had mentioned? Jack figured he would. Tucker was a lot older now than when Jack had last seen him seven years ago, but even in his more youthful days he had had more than his share of spunk and courage. Tucker would do everything he could to make sure Charity was safe. Duke Bryan had put his daughter's safety into good hands.

Duke and Frank walked back inside the ranch house.

Frank sat down on a stool, propping his rifle across his knees.

"Now what?"

"Now we wait. Granger might come soon, might come later. Maybe not at all."

"You really think so? After us bursting out of jail and all?"

"Could be, Jack. Granger's hard to figure. He'll sometimes do the thing you least expect."

"How well do you know Granger?"

"No better than most, I guess. He ain't friendly to just anybody, 'specially to a small rancher like me. He's got power, and he throws it around a lot. I've only talked to him on one or two occasions. He ain't seen too often. He keeps himself holed up at his ranch, away from folks."

"Do you think he'll show up here if his men come after us?"

"I doubt it. He won't expose himself to danger as long as there's others to do it for him. He has more men hired than a lot of the other ranches put together. Some are cattle hands, but a lot are hired guns. That's the way he operates."

There came a faint rustling noise outside in the trees, and in a moment Frank was up and crouched again beside the window. Carefully he looked out through the gap between the split-board shutters.

"See anything?"

"No . . . I think it was the wind. Sure made me jumpy, though."

"You got cause to be jumpy."

Jack took his place beside the other window, staring into the emptiness of a night that gazed back with threatening silence. It would not be long until sunrise. He couldn't decide whether he looked forward to it or dreaded it.

If the three of them had any sense, they would be running across the plains under the cover of night, Jack thought. But he understood Duke's motive for not doing that. If they ran, it would be like giving in to Granger. And it would not be long before other ranchers started doing the same. A lot was riding on Duke Bryan's shoulders right now.

The dawn began breaking in the east, casting an eerie glow over the world, lending a surreal quality to the rolling plains, splitting the sky with golden beams that caught the shimmer of the cottonwood leaves. Then shadows began to appear, long, westward shadows, every second darkening them, intensifying their contrast to the brightening land around them. The dreamlike quality of the world began to fade, the rising sun pouring in the morning steadily.

Jack, Duke, and Frank all stared in silence at the figures outlined on the hill before them, silent figures, slumping carelessly in their saddles, lined up Indian-style against the brightening horizon, wispy clouds of gold and purple visible behind their silhouetted forms. No noise they made, nor any movement, but all in the ranch house could see the flashes of reflected morning light that glinted from the barrels of the Winchesters that lay across their laps.

There was a quiet kind of arrogance in the way Dan Granger's men sat and viewed the scene before them, a deathly kind of calm assurance that what they came to do would be done quickly and in good order. Not a trace of movement could be seen in the line of riders, save for the occasional bending of an elbow to lift a cigarette to a whiskered lip that then sent forth a cloud of smoke to disperse quietly into the morning breeze. How long the riders had been there no one in the ranch house knew; possibly since shortly after Tucker and Charity left.

Duke Bryan whispered a prayer of gratitude that his daughter had made her escape when she did. It would now have been too late.

A burly figure on a big dun stood out in prominence from the group, and after what seemed a torturously long

time, that figure straightened, and a hamlike hand
flipped away the butt of a cheap cigar. Frank recognized
the figure even though the light behind him made his
face invisible. It was Thrasher.

"Bryan! Duke Bryan! We come to get you. You can't
just walk out of a jail! The sheriff is offended. It warn't
good manners!"

Old fool, Frank thought. Old fool really thinks he's
being funny.

There was no answer from the little ranch, only the
calling of a morning bird somewhere in the brush bor-
dering the clearing.

"Bryan, you might as well answer. We know you're
there, and there ain't no point in playing games."

Still no answer.

"Damn it, man, we come to take you back! You got
to stand trial for that rustling charge. You don't want us
to have to come down there and get you. That boy and
that pretty little girl of yours might get hurt!"

A profound sense of relief swept over Duke Bryan.
Thrasher's words told him that Charity and Tucker had
made it past Granger's men without being detected. Apparently the big scoundrel thought Charity was still
here.

"You and your boys had better move on. If the sheriff wants me, he'll have to come for me himself!" Duke
shouted.

Thrasher smiled. "We're doing the sheriff's job for
him, Bryan! We're deputized to bring you back."

"You're loco, Thrasher. You've come for Granger, not
the sheriff. I ain't giving myself up."

Thrasher was grinning even more now. He was enjoying playing this game with Bryan, like a cat toying with
its prey. It would make the taking of him all the more
enjoyable.

Thrasher leaned forward, resting a calloused hand
on his saddlehorn. "Bryan, I'm a fair fellow and a fair

fighter. I'll let you send out your daughter so she don't face no danger when the shooting starts. Otherwise I ain't taking no responsibility for who gets hurt."

Part of Duke Bryan wanted to tell the truth to Thrasher, to flaunt in his face the fact that Charity was already safe, beyond the reach of Granger's treachery, if only for the moment. But he knew it would be best to let the gunmen continue to think she was in the ranch house; if some of them still had a trace of decency left after years of living without regard to conscience, maybe they would be hesitant to attack if they thought their shots might hit a woman.

"I'd sooner send her out into a pack of wolves, Thrasher."

Thrasher shook his head philosophically. "You're a bigger fool than I thought, Bryan. But you've had your chance." The big man looked around him at the stony-faced gunmen. For a tense, long moment there was nerve-eating silence, then Thrasher voiced his command, first softly, then loud and gruff.

"Now . . . NOW!"

The noise of the guns exploding in unison was more like the roar of a cannon than the crackling of individual small arms, and Jack found himself hugging the floor beneath the window before he even realized that he had moved. Ten slugs of lead from ten rifles dug into the wall of the house, one bullet ripping through the hinge of the shutter on Jack's window, causing the shutter to hang askew from its remaining support. Then came more rifle fire, this time not in tandem but instead snapping and cracking in a continuous rhythm, mixed with the sound of horses' hooves on the earth as the riders stormed the house.

Jack forced himself up from the floor and back to the window. The dangling shutter jerked and quivered as another bullet struck it, making a large, splintered hole through it. Jack shoved the shattered piece of wood aside with the muzzle of his rifle and came up firing. A man dropped from the saddle, felled by his bullet. Cold sweat broke out suddenly on Jack's brow, and he felt weak.

Frank and Duke were firing from the other window, both of them bent in concentration, squinting down the barrels of their weapons as they poured a deadly stream of return fire at the riders bearing down on them outside.

Frank followed a hefty man in a wide-brimmed hat with the sight of his Henry, then carefully squeezed the trigger. The man threw his arms to the sky, sending his rifle flying, and tumbled over the rear of his brown stallion to thud into the dirt. Frank didn't watch; he was too busy taking aim on another gunman.

Almost as quickly as they had come, the riders were heading back up the slope, most of them surprised that in one rush they had lost two of their number. The most surprised of all was Thrasher, who sent his horse pounding over the slope of the hill to safety, then stopped long enough to stare numbly at the wound that creased his arm, the skin cut into a long furrow where a bullet had nudged its way past him.

He raged as he watched blood ooze slowly from the wound. With a bearlike roar, he turned his horse around to begin the charge once more.

None of the seven remaining gunmen accompanied their leader. Most had expected to take the house in one rush; none had anticipated such a deadly outpour of fire from the shuttered windows. Thrasher found himself rushing the house alone. With a speed that under other circumstances would have seemed comical, he turned his horse and went speeding up the slope again, three bullets winging past him to inspire increased haste.

Thrasher reined his dun to a stop amid the group of disheartened gunmen, blazing with rage. He spit out a long string of invectives, his face growing redder and his frown more bitter. "Are you going to leave me to take that ranch myself?"

"Thrasher, you saw what happened—them folks down there is crack shots. We rush again, and two or three more of us will be gone."

"You explain that to Granger when he asks you, why ten of the territory's top guns couldn't take four men and a girl! He'll be real interested in hearing you explain that!"

"Thrasher, settle down. Perry's right. Rushing the house ain't the way to do it." The speaker was a tall man in a dusty brown hat and leather vest. He had a rather large, thin nose, deep-set eyes, and craggy features that suggested a distorted handsomeness. He was Mick Brandon, who had carved out a reputation as a fast gun as many a greenhorn had carved out his own epitaph trying to prove he was faster. Brandon was a quiet man, generally, and one Thrasher didn't like, for when he spoke, the others tended to listen. In his slow brain, Thrasher sensed that Brandon was his better both mentally and physically, and it angered him. He wouldn't do anything about it, though—he was far too scared of Brandon's fast gun hand.

"What are you suggesting, Brandon?"

"Burn 'em out! When we're riding down on 'em, they got the advantage, 'cause we can't shoot accurately, and they can aim good and steady. Rushing ain't the thing to do. We gotta burn 'em out."

Thrasher stared icily at the lean gunman, dropping his gaze suddenly when Brandon returned the stare. Speaking low, almost glumly, he said, "I got a little bottle of coal oil in my saddlebag for campfires. We can use it to fuel some torches."

Chapter 9

The waiting was the worst part, the uncertainty about what Thrasher and his men were up to, the assurance that no matter how complete the silence, the battle was not over. Jack and his two companions sat at their window positions until the waiting became unbearable, then they stood and began walking about the room, trying to ease the tension with movement and conversation.

"Could they have left, Pa? I don't think they were expecting this much resistance."

"No, I don't think they'll leave until they've got us one way or the other. I can't blame 'em. I hear Granger is a hard man to deal with when he don't get what he wants, and what he wants is us."

Jack walked toward the rear of the building. "It's too bad you didn't put windows on this part of the house. We could see if they came up from behind."

Duke slapped his thigh impatiently. "Blast it! I know they're up to something."

"I know what you mean, Mr. Bryan."

"Call me Duke. I never did take to the mister stuff. I'm going to get me some coffee. Anybody want some?"

The idea was appealing, for it injected a bit of the routine into the tense situation. Jack and Frank brightened at the offer. Duke opened the door to the cast-iron oven and tossed in a couple of logs. The fire blazed brighter; he shut the door and adjusted the round eye of the stove with a detachable iron handle. Soon the coffee was boiling in a speckled-blue tin pot, filling the little cabin with a tantalizing aroma. Jack returned to his window, peeking out around the demolished shutter to see if there was sign of any renewed attack. Frank came to him and thrust a tin mug of coffee into his hand, and he began sipping the strong and steaming brew, his eyes studying the horizon.

There was no sign of life, no trace of man or horse to betray the presence of Granger's riders—nothing but brilliant blue of the sky, now lit with the full glory of morning, the billowing heaps of snowy clouds high overhead, the faint movement of the breeze-whipped cottonwoods, the thin, white curl of smoke from over the hill . . .

Smoke?

Jack set the mug of coffee on a stool nearby and gazed with a frown at the curling smoke. It appeared to be coming from just over the crest of the slope, in the general area of where he expected the riders to be.

It could only mean one thing. He called for Duke.

"What is it, Jack?"

Jack gestured toward the thin band of rising smoke. Duke looked at it for a long time, then whistled between his teeth.

"That does it for us. They get this place on fire, and we're goners."

"Fire? What's happening, Pa?"

"They got fire up there, and something tells me it ain't to cook their breakfast. Fire's the one thing I was hoping they wouldn't think of."

Jack looked out the window again, silent. For a moment all his hopes seemed to drift away with the wispy smoke he was watching, but suddenly a strong urge to live flowed through him, no matter what.

"Duke, we can't stay here," he said.

Duke nodded. "Just what I was thinking. Frank, go open up the trap."

"The trap? What do you mean?" asked Jack.

"When we were putting the floorboards in this

place, we came up short on a section, so we just built us a small kind of door to cover it. I figured in cold weather we could just stack up firewood under the house right beneath the door and get it in without having to get our feet cold. Never really used it, though. Got a piece of furniture on top of it right now."

The three men moved into the dog trot, heading for the boarded-up rear wall. A large wardrobe sat there, well-stuffed with old clothing and linens. Frank and his father began hefting the heavy piece to the side. In moments they had exposed a large trapdoor hidden beneath it.

"Well, men, here goes!" exclaimed Duke, reaching for the leather thong that served as a handle for the door. Before he threw it open, he paused, sending Frank scurrying back into the main room to gather all the spare ammunition. The young man came back with hands and pockets stuffed with shells, which he quickly distributed to the others.

Duke threw open the trapdoor then, a rush of fresh air filling the passageway. There was nothing beneath the door but a few scraps of discarded firewood and a rounded hollow in the bare earth where the Bryans' old hound had made a sleeping place in the shady coolness under the cabin.

Jack started to lower himself through the opening, but he was stopped by a low growl from beneath the house as well as the touch of Duke's hand on his shoulder.

"Here—let me or Frank go first. Ol' Rex will raise a ruckus if you go through, you being a stranger to him and all."

Jack climbed back up and made way for Duke, who quickly scrambled down through the trapdoor and onto the ground. Rex came sniffing and wagging his tail around his master, who quickly patted him to keep him from making noise.

"Easy, boy. Just stay quiet."

Frank followed his father out the opening. Jack exited last. Crouching to avoid bumping their heads on the bottom of the cabin floorboards, they moved toward the rear of the building.

Then they stood outside, the house between them and the hill that hid the eight riders. Jack looked to Duke for the next move, having no idea what to do. If even one of the riders caught sight of them outside the protection of the cabin, they would likely be run down and shot, or perhaps captured and hanged.

"We got to have horses," Duke said.

"We'll have to run the clearing between here and the stable," said Frank. "If they see us . . ."

"What choice do we have?"

Jack looked across the clearing, a bare piece of ground beaten flat and hard by the hooves of horses. The area through which they would have to run was small— no more than a hundred feet across at the most—but with eight angry gunmen just across the hill, possibly even now watching the house for sign of movement, the distance seemed vast, formidable.

Jack adjusted his hat and shrugged his shoulders, trying to put on a casual front. "Well, men . . . let's run!"

And run they did. Keeping their heads low, fearing to look to their left up the hill and into the face of possible death, they sprinted across the clearing.

The dark stable loomed up before them. Jack pounded inside, not stopping until his hands touched the opposite wall. He had made it. Not a shot fired.

"I can't believe it!" Frank exclaimed.

From the hill came the sound of rushing hooves. Jack and his companions ducked farther back into the darkness of the stable, then carefully peered out through the open doorway.

A rider was bearing down on the house at full speed, crouched low in the saddle, his hand grasping a flaring torch. Within fifty feet of the house he rode—Jack couldn't help but admire his daring—and the torch became an arching bow of yellow against the blue of the sky as he heaved it to the wood-shingled roof of the house.

"When I think how long it took to build that place, how hard I worked, how many memories . . ."

Jack glanced over at Duke. The man's eyes showed a curious combination of wistfulness and anger. This wasn't going to be just any fire. A life of dreams and labor were going to be destroyed in those flames. Duke was fairly new to the Montana Territory, and the house had only sat there for about two years, but there had been a lifetime of planning and sweating invested in it, all now to be robbed by roaring flames and the inexplicable wrath of the mysterious Dan Granger.

The dry shingles began to smolder; the torch lay flaring on the rooftop, wavy swirls of heat distorting upward. Then came another horseman, and another torch thrown upward. Duke Bryan fingered the butt of his rifle, bit his lip, but did nothing.

Jack realized that their escape attempt had come too late. With the mounted gunmen again in view of the house and stable, they were just as trapped as before. All they could do was watch the flames spread across the roof, steadily growing, crackling and sending a multiplying shower of sparks to the sky.

"In a minute they're going to start wondering why we aren't coming out or at least shooting at 'em," said Frank. "What should we do, Pa?"

"I tell you one thing—we can't sit and wait for them to find us," Duke said. The embittered rancher swung his rifle to his shoulder, his burly hand swinging the lever and pumping a new slug home. He lined up his sights on one of the riders who was bearing down on the ranch house to throw a fresh torch through one of the open windows.

The stable echoed with the roar of the gun. The rider jerked in his saddle and fell sidelong to the earth, his hand still gripping the torch even as he writhed on the dirt. Then Duke's rifle spoke again, and another rider cried out in terror as a high-powered slug ripped through the crown of his hat, missing his head by a fraction of an inch.

Duke's spirit touched off a spark of life within Jack, arousing his fighting instinct, making him desire to sell his life as dearly as possible, if sell it he must. He dropped on one knee, raised his weapon, and joined his fire with that of the rancher. Frank took a position on the other side of the stable door and opened up with a stream of deadly, steady fire as well.

Granger's riders disappeared quickly, stunned to find themselves endangered from a new direction, confused about how the men they thought were trapped in a burning house had managed to miraculously travel to the nearby stable. Thrasher raced his dun over the crest of the slope as a bullet winged by his left ear.

There again was silence, tense and threatening. The three fighters in the stable took the opportunity to reload their hot weapons, then stood listening for any hint of further attack.

The silence continued, eating into their nerves. At last Jack began to suspect that their unexpected blitz from the stable had broken the nerve of the attackers and sent them on their way.

Then came a quiet kind of hissing noise from the opposite side of the stable. Confused, Jack turned to look at the others and found them staring at something in the stable's loft.

The loft was in flames, the straw burning hot and bright and spreading quickly around the torch that had been tossed in through the single ventilation window in the stable. This torch had apparently been tossed not by a rider but by a man on foot, who had stealthily crept over the slope out of view of the stable's occupants.

"They've got us, boys," Duke said in a dull tone. Filled with a sudden courage born of desperation, Jack leaped outside the stable and began pumping a deadly rain of lead up the slope.

Jack was driven back inside as dirt began kicking up

around his heels. Levering his rifle, he sent a futile shot winging up the slope as a final defiant gesture.

Frank had already scrambled into the loft, a saddle blanket in his hands. Bravely he began beating at the flames as his father followed him up the ladder, Jack at his heels.

Duke grabbed another blanket and began working beside his son. The air was a choking mixture of burning straw fragments, smoke, and lung-searing heat. Jack grabbed up his rifle and dug into his pocket for ammunition. Ducking the dangerous exposure of the window, he moved over to the opposite side. He sighted down the length of the muzzle at the faint, fleeing forms he could make out atop the hill and began firing.

Duke and Frank were choking, coughing, occasionally having to stop their seemingly fruitless battling of the flames in order to beat out fire that set into their clothes. The heat grew intense, the air smoke-filled. Though the two firefighters continually beat at the flames, they were losing the battle. In a matter of minutes the stable would be as engulfed in flame as was the flaring, roaring inferno of the ranch house just across the clearing.

Jack wiped sweat from a grimy brow and kept pumping bullets into the distance, the smoke whipping about him, burning into his eyes. Return fire ripped into the log walls about him, close shots occasionally whipping past his head to implant themselves in the opposite wall.

Granger's riders emerged from their refuge in the trees and brush across the hill, riding hard, moving straight toward the stable.

This was it. The final attack, the last rush. In moments the riders would be upon them, and with the finality of a few blasts from their Winchesters, it would be over. Jack emptied the chamber of his rifle and prepared for death.

And then, miraculously, unbelievably, the riders veered to the right, past the barn, running as if the devil himself were on their tails.

Over the crest of the hill appeared a new band of riders, guns blazing, horses running, pursuing the fleeing band of Granger's gunmen.

Chapter 10

Jack joined with Frank and his father in trying to beat out the flames, lashing out at them with a horse blanket, unable to take time even to query Duke about the new riders.

The flames began to lose their hold in the stable. But there was no hope for the house; it was now a smoldering shell, a red-hot skeleton of a building that looked as if a slight wind would bowl it over.

A handful of men entered the open doorway to the stable, and Duke said: "Buck—I'm glad to see you! Quick! Help me save the barn. The house . . ."

"The house is gone, Duke," said a pudgy man in a red-checked shirt and a wide-brimmed slouch hat. He was climbing the ladder to the loft, one burly hand grasping the wooden rungs, the other clinging to a Henry that still was exuding a wispy swirl of thin smoke from the rim of the muzzle.

Duke bit his lip and started whipping at the flames with renewed fervor. The man named Buck took off his leather vest and joined the others, two other men coming up the ladder behind him and adding their efforts to the battle as well.

Little by little the flames died away. Duke treaded out the last remaining fragments of burning straw with his boot. He turned and extended his hand to Buck. His face looked weary, sad, yet tremendously relieved.

"Buck—if you hadn't showed up, I guess we'd either be roasted or shot by now. But how did you know?"

"I didn't. Or I should say, *we* didn't. But we did

know that you had got out of the jail, and it wasn't hard to guess what would happen. I'm just sorry it took so long for us to get here. Some of the ranches are spread out pretty far, you know, and we had to ride hard. We're all plenty worried about what Granger is trying to do to you. If you go, then our ranches go next."

The group descended from the loft and walked into the open air, the smell and taste of hot smoke and sweat clinging to them. Duke looked bitter when he saw what little was left of his log home, even now crumbling away as the flames ate away the last remaining supports that held up the charred roof.

"No matter what, I can't deny that Granger has won part of his battle right here," he said. "There's something gone that can never be replaced. I can rebuild the house, but something will be different. There will be the memory of what was here before, and how I lost it."

The stocky leader of the group approached Jack and thrust out his hand. Jack took it and pumped it firmly. "Buck Treadway."

"Jack Corrigan. Pleased to meet you—more pleased than you might know."

The big man laughed, his eyes disappearing into a sea of wrinkles. "You fellers were in something of a fix!"

"And we still are, if you ask me. And you, too, Buck," Frank cut in. "Dan Granger won't let this pass. He'll be after all of you, too."

"Let him come," said Treadway, his voice now as cold as it was jovial a moment before. "This thing calls for a response from us—we've let it go long enough. We have rights here just as much as Granger, and it's high time we stood up for 'em."

Duke turned away from the flaming remains of his home. "What now, Buck? Where can we go? Granger will have more men on us than we can hope to handle if we stay here. And if we go to any other ranch, it will just wind up like mine—burnt to the ground."

"You got a point, Duke. Maybe we ought to have us

a quick meeting. We'll let the group decide what to do next."

The idea sounded reasonable. Jack was introduced to the group, slapped on the back by about two dozen hands, while congratulations and praise were poured upon him. The ranchers introduced themselves one by one, but hardly had they finished before Jack promptly forgot them all, his mind still spinning from the tumult of the battle.

The meeting took place before the grove of trees that lined the slope facing the ranch. The ranchers sat in a circle on the ground, some crouched on their haunches like Indians, others seated cross-legged with rifles across their laps. Most had cigars or pipes thrust into their mouths, and all looked deadly serious about what they were doing. No one was anxious to submit to a man like Granger, yet none of them would be happy to expose their ranches to danger.

Buck Treadway stood in the midst of the group and looked around him. "Men, you know the situation," he said. "You can see from what Granger did to Duke's ranch how far he will go when he's angry. We got to go somewhere. We've set our course. I don't like risking my home and cattle just to spite Dan Granger. But on the other hand, I ain't willing to turn tail in front of him."

"What are you getting at, Buck?" asked a thin man in a ragged blue shirt.

"That maybe the thing to do ain't to turn tail, but to take on Granger face-to-face."

The words brought stunned silence for a moment, then Duke spoke. "You mean make a raid on Granger's ranch?"

"Not exactly. Better to talk out every angle of a thing before fighting it out. It's never crossed our minds that Granger might be willing to listen to reason. Maybe if we talk to him . . ."

"It won't work, Buck. Granger won't talk to us."

"He's right, Buck," someone else chimed in.

Treadway raised his hand to quiet the voices. "You don't know what he might do. Nobody has tried to reason with the man before and maybe that's been a mistake. I can't guarantee that it won't blow up in our face, but even that seems better to me than waiting for him to come to us when he feels like it."

Duke nodded. "I think I see your point, Buck. If we wait around and do nothing, Granger's men will attack when it's best for them. But if we move in when they don't expect it . . ."

"Then we'll have the advantage. Maybe Granger will be willing to talk it out and settle things."

One man spit a wad of tobacco on the ground and shook his head. "I still ain't convinced, Buck. A man trying to keep from getting snake-bit shouldn't stick his foot into the den."

"We ain't just going to waltz in there and let Granger have his way with us, Bill. We'll be armed and ready to fight if need be."

"I still don't like the idea."

"I understand that . . . but do you have any better ones?"

The man's heavy brows drooped low over deep-set eyes. He shifted the wad of tobacco from one side of his mouth to the other, then shrugged. "I reckon not."

"What do you say then? Are you with me?"

Buck looked at the circle of faces, waiting for a response. And he got one, though not in words. Every man gave a slight nod, a twitch of the finger, or some other faint gesture that let him know his plan was accepted. Buck smiled faintly, then thrust his hands into his pockets and jutted out his prominent belly.

"All right, then. We'll go to Granger's."

Jack's skin was crawling. He saw the sense in what Buck had suggested, but the idea of another possible confrontation with Granger's men was frightening. And he was beginning to think of Tucker again, and his father back in Wyoming.

In the excitement of battle Jack had almost forgotten about his father's illness and the pressing need to finish this business and get back to the ranch on the Crazy Woman. He had no desire to see the defense of the small ranchers crumble under Granger's chastening, and he felt a personal stake in it all due to the likely presence of Thurston Russell in the area. But still there was his own family responsibility to think about. And after all, he had already done more than his part to help out Duke.

As the informal meeting broke up, Duke walked over to Jack's side.

"I appreciate all you've done," he said. "As far as I'm concerned, you're free to go home."

Jack smiled weakly. His mind was full of conflict. Emotion pulled him southward toward home while a sense of duty to finish what he had started made him want to stay here. What to do? He wished he could find the answer easily.

"I don't really know what I ought to do, Duke."

"Of course you do. You've got a responsibility to your father. That's important."

"So is what you're doing. And if our roles were reversed, I'd like to think somebody would care enough to help me fight it out."

Duke patted Jack's shoulder. "You can leave when you want, or stay. It's your choice and I won't push you about it. But there'll be no hard feelings if you go. Think about it."

Jack did think about it, and the more he did the more he was inclined to leave. He had no business getting more deeply involved in this fight, risking his life while his father waited for him back home.

But thinking of his father suddenly made him recall a time when they were together. Jack had been twelve years old, and he and his father had just sold a few head of cattle and were returning from herding them to the pickup point for the buyer. They stopped at a café and ordered a meal. When they were finished with it, they left, and on the way back to the horses passed a saloon.

At that moment the door had burst open and a man had fallen out onto his back. Danver had to sweep Jack aside to keep him from being crushed beneath the fellow.

"Hey now, watch it around my boy!" Danver exclaimed.

The man stood. His lip was bleeding. He turned a crimson scowl on Danver but said nothing; his mind was still fixed on whatever had happened inside the saloon. Jack wasn't even sure the man was really aware of them, distracted as he was.

Another man came to the door. "We'll have no putrid Irish about here," he said. "You drink at your own slop pits and stay away from a decent man's saloon."

The bleeding Irishman snarled and bolted toward the saloon door, but the man inside slammed it shut. The Irishman faltered, hesitated between decisions a few moments, then at last turned away, muttering.

"Hang, draw, and quarter the damnable lot of them," he said in a thick brogue. "I'd sooner drink with a heathen Chinee when it comes down to it. I'll not drink where a good man's treated like a swine."

Only then did he apparently truly notice Danver and Jack. He had looked right through them before. His broad face grew red in obvious embarrassment. He wiped away blood from his lip. "I'm sorry indeed," he said. "I had a bit of a row and did not mean to intrude upon you."

Danver gestured at the saloon. "Irish not welcome, I gather."

"The proprietor seems to have a bit of a problem with such as myself, yes."

Jack was intrigued with the man, who looked and sounded to him like the essence of everything Irish. The fellow looked quizzically at Danver. "And what is your attitude on the subject, sir?" he asked in a slightly challenging tone. Jack wondered if maybe the man was looking for someone to fight to vent his fresh humiliation.

"My name is Danver Corrigan, sprung from the O'Corrigans, so what do you think?"

A broad grin spread across the broader face. The Irishman slapped a hand as big as a steak on Danver's shoulder. "Riley's my name, friend Corrigan. Glad to meet you. Did you come straight from the old land itself?"

"No, but my grandfather did, bringing my father with him," Danver returned.

Riley looked down at Jack. "And this would be your lad?"

Danver introduced Jack, who thrust up his hand and then tried not to wince as Riley crushed it in greeting.

Riley wiped some fresh blood that had risen on his damaged lip and said, "Sorry again to have bothered you, my friends. Yet I'm glad to have met you, for seeing one's own always brightens the sunshine a bit, but I'll be on my way now."

"Not yet, not yet. When two Irishmen meet they ought at least to raise a glass together."

Riley looked interested but uncertain. "You mean in there?" he asked, thumbing toward the saloon.

"There indeed."

Jack looked up at his father with wide eyes. "But Pa . . ."

"No buts, Son." Danver looked at Riley with his eyes twinkling. "Except maybe a few we might have to kick inside that saloon."

Riley's eyes caught the same gleam. "Aye, friend Corrigan. Indeed."

Danver looked down at Jack. "Not a word to your mother, hear? And if anything rowdy begins, it's out the door with you."

Jack nodded. His heart beat more quickly. Excitement stole over him and he smiled.

He was a little disappointed later when they left without having had a fight. Jumping one half-drunken Irishman was one thing for the Irish-hating barkeep and his cronies; jumping two of them, when one was so stout a man as Danver Corrigan, was another. The barroom rowdies had merely skulked in the corner, glaring their hatred at the two Irishmen until they were through. Danver doffed his hat and tipped the bartender five cents as he left.

"Spend it wisely, good friend," he said in his best imitation of his Irish-born father.

Later Danver talked to Jack about what he had done. "It wasn't a matter of needing or wanting a drink, nor of looking for a fight," he said. "It's just that a man can't walk away when he encounters a thing that is wrong, particularly an injustice against another. He has to step in and make it his business to set things right, or do his best to. That's the way of the Corrigans."

Jack looked across at Duke Bryan. Duke's situation was not much different, in a way, than that of Riley the Irishman. He was being trodden upon for no good reason. Being done an injustice.

Jack then knew why he was staying. It was because of what his father had told him so many years back. A man could not walk away from an injustice. Especially when the man was a Corrigan.

Jack heard a rushing of hooves on the earth and turned to see three of the ranchers heading westward toward one of the nearby ranches, probably to pick up more ammunition before the move toward Granger's ranch.

The group decided to wait until dawn to approach Granger's home. Feelings at the Circle X would be hot now in the aftermath of the unsuccessful move on the Bryan ranch, and a cooling-off period might greatly enhance the chances of a peaceful settlement, the men decided.

The three riders returned some hours later with ammunition and food. Eating a hearty meal, the group made camp on the Bryan ranch grounds. Jack made out his bedroll with the conviction that he would get no sleep, then lay down and immediately dropped into an exhausted, dreamless slumber.

Chapter 11

Tucker rode through the darkness, convinced he had done the wrong thing in leaving Charity alone in the line camp. What would Duke think when he came riding in, strictly against orders, leaving Charity alone and virtually defenseless in an abandoned cabin ten miles away?

Tucker felt guilty but kept riding. It had been a full day since he and Charity had set out from the ranch; surely Granger's men had come by now if they were coming at all. Still, Tucker hoped he was not too late to give any help that might be needed.

It was almost pitch-black on the plains, the pale and misty moonlight giving the only illumination of the empty land. The plains seemed to swallow that thin light, drinking it in as if thirsty for it.

He recognized from the lay of the land that he was approaching the area of the ranch. Catching his breath in his throat and feeling a sudden racing of his pulse, he came to the top of the ridge and looked down at what lay beyond.

The barn was there, faintly outlined in the moonlight, standing as it always had at the perimeter of the ranch clearing. But the house . . .

A faint red glow rose from the smoldering coals that lay where the house had been. It was gone, entirely gone, burned right down to the foundation stones. Tucker's heart sank. His pulse pounded at his throat. Immediately there came to mind an image of his father, lying there in his deathbed at the Crazy Woman ranch, waiting for Tucker to return with a young man he had not seen for seven years, a son perhaps now destined to never return.

Tucker feared Jack was dead. He morbidly wondered if his brother had died with a bullet in his head or a noose around his neck.

His head hanging, he moved down the dark and silent slope toward the smoldering corpse of a house that sent forth a faint red glow into the darkness. Tucker didn't know just what he was searching for. Maybe nothing. But he wanted to be close to the place where he felt sure Jack had died.

Tucker brought his horse to a halt and dismounted. Silently he strode toward the remains of the house, then he stopped and knelt down into the dirt.

His fingers traced a line in the dirt, and he noticed the marks of horses' hooves in the soft earth. He looked around. There were hoof marks everywhere, as if maybe as many as two dozen horses had thundered through the area. Granger's men must have been a powerful force.

He stood and walked back to his waiting horse. The animal was tired, covered with a thin lather, but he would work it more this night. He was filled with a bitter desire to look into the eyes of a man who could order the murder of men who had in no way wronged him.

But Tucker had no idea where Granger's ranch lay. Mounting his horse, he sat in the saddle for a moment, thinking.

There were other ranches to the east. He had noticed a handful of them as they rode here to Duke's ranch the night before. Surely someone there would know where Dan Granger's spread was.

Turning his back on the ranch of Duke Bryan, Tucker spurred his horse to a trot and disappeared into the night.

Charity Bryan sat silent in the darkness, watching the first hint of morning light tint the eastern horizon. As the light grew, so did her fears.

She had reached the borders of Granger's ranch some two hours before, coming as close as she dared to the main house, knowing the rancher kept the place closely guarded, like a fortress.

In a sense that was exactly what it was, she thought. Granger was a man with a reputation as an eccentric, one who generally baffled most people. Partly the stories about him were fiction, Charity figured, tales wrought out of people's curiosity about a man who kept himself holed up alone in a large ranch house, separated from contact with his fellow humans, seen publicly only in the company of some of his hired gun hands or the sheriff everyone knew he controlled. The rare occasions when any of the townsfolk caught sight of Dan Granger in public generally became the topics of conversation in the cafés and saloons, the places where the legends multiplied and grew about the unknowable rancher.

Charity had heard the stories—how Granger would never suffer a woman to enter his home, how mere contact with one made him grow angry.

But Charity knew better. If what Seth Bailey had told her in dying gasps was true, then Dan Granger was capable of at least some feeling toward a woman. She shuddered.

Charity had made no move toward the ranch in the darkness, for the guards she felt certain were at the place would have made short work of her. Whether an approach in the daylight would be any safer she did not know, but she was determined to try. Maybe if she could confront Granger and talk to him, he would leave her father alone. She tried not to think about the possibility it might already be too late.

The light broke on a clear morning, streaming across the prairie and revealing the ranch house that had before been shrouded in darkness. The building was a far cry from the usual low, dirt-roofed log sheds that most local ranchers lived in. Charity knew that her father had taken special pains with their house, hewing the logs

square and taking the time to build a shingle roof, but his
and every other ranch house she had seen paled in comparison to that of Dan Granger.

The house was a two-story log building, three gables
breaking through the roof of uniform shingles. The logs
were so straight and evenly notched as to require almost
no chinking, and two large stone chimneys graced both
ends of the house. A rail fence surrounded a spacious
yard on all sides of the structure. Flanking the yard on
the sides and rear were several buildings, ranging from a
large log barn to smaller sod structures. Standing to one
side was a huge bunkhouse built of rough, hand-sawed
lumber. Between the bunkhouse and the ranch house
was a smaller building that Charity guessed to be the
kitchen.

There was no sign of movement around the ranch
save for the scuffling and shifting of a handful of chickens
and the lazy loping of a dog toward the bunkhouse. The
sun illuminated the scene through a cool-morning at-
mosphere touched with just a hint of dew. Such was the
serenity of the entire panorama that for a moment
Charity almost forgot that within the walls of that massive, impenetrable home lived a man who was doing his
best to see her father dead.

She stood gazing upon the ranch from the safety of
distance until the sun was well risen over the eastern
horizon. Her horse grazed a short distance away in a concealing grove of scrubby trees, rested after the long ride
from the deserted line camp. Steeling herself for the or-
deal to come, Charity walked toward the horse. Mounting, she moved from the concealment of the trees and
down the narrow dirt road that led to the opulent home.

Even now she had been spotted, she guessed. She
didn't care; she wanted Granger's guards to see her long
before she rode within close range of their rifles. She
wanted them to know that she was making no attempt at
covert action. Most of all, she wanted them to know that
she was a woman. Though Granger was rumored to hate

women—the result of a jilting, she had heard—maybe his guard had enough respect for her sex to let her pass safely.

The road to the house seemed extremely long. With every slow, probing step of her horse's hooves Charity counted the seconds. She kept her eyes focused on the house as she rode, unwilling to look to either side for fear of what she might see. She was sure she was being watched now; she had seen the faint movement of one of the pale curtains that hung shroudlike inside the windows.

Charity was within two hundred feet of the house when two men approached, coming from either side of the building, rifles in their hands. She stopped, her breath coming faster. For a long time the men stood regarding her with cold, unreadable expressions, then the taller of the two spoke. He had a rough, grinding voice that grated on her nerves like the scales of a dead fish rubbing flesh.

"Who are you, and what is your business?"

Charity swallowed. "My name's Charity Bryan. I've come to see Mr. Granger."

The tall man glanced at his partner. "Bryan?"

"That's right. My father is Duke Bryan. I'm sure you've heard of him."

The man said nothing, glancing again at his partner, then asked, "Why do you want to see Mr. Granger?"

Charity sat up straight in the saddle, trying to put on an air of confidence and authority. "This is between Mr. Granger and me."

The shorter guard spoke. He had a high, almost effeminate voice that seemed out of harmony with his stocky build. "Don't get sassy, little lady. We got orders to turn away anybody that ain't invited here, no questions asked."

"I think when you tell Mr. Granger who I am, he will want to see me."

"She's right. I do."

The voice came in conjunction with the opening of the heavy front door. The guards moved a couple of steps backward, turning toward the doorway.

A man of medium height and weight, clean-shaven except for a pair of thick, graying sideburns that contrasted with the darkness of his slightly long and wavy hair, stood in the doorway, looking upon the lovely young lady mounted bravely before him. His face was ruggedly handsome, with deep brown eyes beneath expressive eyebrows, a noble-looking nose, and thin, firmly set lips setting off his features with an air of dignity and power. He was dressed in a loose robe of lavender, tied at his waist and hanging almost to his ankles. In his hand was a curved pipe, and he fingered it as he looked at Charity with his dark, expressive eyes.

It was the first time Charity Bryan had ever laid eyes on the famed Dan Granger. Somehow what she saw was not what she had expected. Granger didn't look like the epitome of evil. He looked like a man who could comfortably wear a ministerial collar. Charity had always paid a lot of attention to her first impressions of those she met, and her impression of Dan Granger was so totally at odds with what she had expected that for a time she was speechless.

Granger seemed in no hurry to speak further himself. He regarded Charity for a long time before he again spoke in a voice as smooth as fresh cream.

"So you are Duke Bryan's daughter. I'll admit you're one sight I never expected to see. And I'm surprised that Bryan raised such a lovely child—even if she is a bit immodest."

Charity ignored the obvious reference to her exposed legs, though she suddenly was painfully conscious of the eyes of the two guards upon her. Refusing to break the gaze she held upon Granger, she cleared her throat and tried not to sound nervous.

"I've come to talk to you about my father, Mr. Granger. May I come in?"

Granger looked down then, producing a match from the pocket of his robe. Striking it on the doorpost, he lit his pipe, concentrating on the flame touching the tobacco. His expression was calm, masking his discomfort in the presence of the young woman. For she reminded him of another woman he had known, and the memory stung.

Dan Granger drew in a cloud of smoke and exhaled it into the dewy light of the morning. He stepped back into the doorway.

"By all means, Miss Bryan, do come in. Make yourself comfortable while I go upstairs to dress."

Charity dismounted. One of the guards moved forward to take the reins of the horse. The door shut behind Charity.

Chapter 12

Charity sat in a fancy, engraved mahogany chair atop a plush velvet cushion, looking around her, feeling out of place and scared.

Granger had ascended the stairs to dress, he said, and Charity could do nothing at present but await his return. In a way she dreaded it, for she had no clear idea of just what to say to the man. She hoped it would not be necessary to confront him with what Seth Bailey had told her the night he died.

Granger descended the stairs, trailing a cloud of pipe smoke. He was dressed in a well-cut suit, obviously tailor-made. He was a handsome and dashing figure, even more so than before. Charity's nervousness doubled.

Granger sat down in a cushioned chair across from her and studied her with his expressive eyes. Charity felt like a piece of beef hanging in a butcher's window.

"You are a very pretty young lady, Miss Bryan. Very pretty. Even features, graceful of form . . . a bit sunburned, perhaps, but—"

"Thank you, sir." Charity didn't want to hear more.

"You're very welcome." He took several leisurely puffs from his pipe. "Tell me . . . are you surprised that I let you in here?"

"I . . . I'm not sure what you mean, sir."

"Oh, come now—surely you've heard the stories, about how I never let a female set foot in my house. I hear some view me as quite a strange character. Probably think I make human sacrifices and eat babies for supper."

Charity could think of nothing to say to that, so she simply sat, staring blankly at the pipe-smoking rancher. She had a vague maddening feeling that the man was trying to unnerve her.

Granger stood and moved toward the window, looking out across the plains. Morning light streamed around him and revealed flecks of almost invisible dust floating in the air. At last he turned toward her.

"I assume you had a reason for coming here."

"Yes."

"Well?"

"You had my father jailed on false charges, Mr. Granger. And you've had your men harassing him. I came to ask you to stop." Charity forced out the words as fast as she could, hoping her voice would not falter.

Granger looked at her with the expression of an innocent child accused of stealing candy. "Miss Bryan, I have nothing against your father at all, and I'm sorry you think that I do. I haven't tried to harass him in any way. About his being jailed—well, two of my best men swore they found him rustling my cattle. What else could I do? A man has to protect what is his. I'm sure your father would have done the same."

Charity's courage was bolstered by anger. Granger was playing a game with her, toying with her words. She gritted her teeth, glaring at him in rage.

"Don't try to bluff me, Mr. Granger. Both of us know what you have been doing. You've sought every chance to hurt my father, and both of us know he had nothing to do with any rustling of your cattle. He's never done a thing to interfere with your business—he's never given you any trouble at all. Yet you've continually harassed him in spite of that, again and again. All we want is to be left alone—that's not too much to ask, is it? Why can't you just call off your men and leave my father alone?"

Granger smiled, a faint, teasing smile. "I have to admit I'm mystified by what you say, Miss Bryan. I can't imagine why you would think I have been deliberately harassing your father. So, certainly there's nothing I can do to stop whatever trouble he might be having."

Charity felt exasperation rising. Granger obviously was going to continue this verbal cat-and-mouse until the end. He wasn't interested in reasoning with her.

Granger stood up and walked over to the window, puffing his pipe. "Look out there, Miss Bryan. That's a big land, a vast one. There's room enough for all of us— myself, your father, almost any number of ranchers. I have no hard feelings toward your father or any other rancher. But he was caught rustling, and when a man steals from another, he has to pay the price. It bothers me that you seem to think I'm evil just because I seek to enforce the laws against rustling. I'm not the kind of man to . . ."

Something snapped inside Charity. Rising up like a whirlwind, she lashed out at the arrogant rancher.

"I know what kind of man you are, Dan Granger. You don't have to play games with me. You don't hate my father because you think he's a rustler—you know as well as I that he isn't. You hate my father because he is the man who was married to a lady your sick mind found attractive—so attractive that you broke into her home one night while she was alone and tried to force yourself on her. I know what kind of man you are. You're the kind that hates women and longs for them at the same time. You're the kind that can only relate to a woman the way you relate to all other people—as a thing to be used for your own pleasure. You're an evil man, Granger, and I hate you for what you tried to do to my mother and what you are doing to my father. I hate you!"

Granger turned a dark stare upon the young woman. "Why, you little—"

"Shut up. I won't listen to you. But you're going to hear me out. I know what you tried to do to my mother—I know because I was told by the man that tore you away from her and sent you whimpering back to your ranch. And you so drunk that you never even knew who it was! It was Seth Bailey, Mr. Granger, and it can't hurt him for you to know that now, because he's dead. He told me about it before he died, and now I understand what it is that drives you to torment my father like you do.

"You can't stand it that my father enjoyed a normal, happy life with my mother as long as she lived, can you? It eats away at you, doesn't it? You don't want control of the small ranches around here—that's what everyone says you want, but I know better. All you want is to act out your revenge on my father . . . because he had the privilege of living a happy life with the woman you wanted for yourself."

Granger leaped at Charity, his face livid. He cursed through gritted teeth. Charity nimbly leaped away from the rancher, and he sprawled suddenly on the floor. The young lady backed up against a table that stood against the wall, holding glasses and bottles of expensive liquor.

Granger rose and came at her again. As he lunged forward, Charity's grasp closed on a bottle of whiskey on the table behind her. She leaped aside as the rancher reached her, and he crashed into the table, sending glasses and liquor flying as it overturned.

Charity swung the bottle she was holding by the neck at the back of the chair where Granger had been sitting minutes before. The bottle smashed, leaving her with the broken neck in her hand, the jagged edges as sharp and deadly as any knife.

Cursing, Granger again rose and moved toward her. Charity screamed and blindly lashed out with her makeshift weapon.

Granger cried out and drew back a hand bloody and torn. Charity went pale. Granger stared first at the bleeding hand, then at the young lady. Then, raising his face toward the ceiling, he sent forth a ringing cry.

The door burst open and the two guards appeared, rifles in hand. Confused, they stared at the wounded rancher's bleeding hand, uncertain about what had happened and what they should do.

"Grab her!" screamed Granger. "Hold her!"

Charity darted toward the door, swinging the broken bottle at the guards. But the men managed to deflect the thrust, and Charity was grasped in strong, muscled hands, the bottle knocked from her grasp.

Granger gripped his bleeding hand and walked to where Charity struggled in the grasp of the burly gunmen. The rancher stood before her and smiled.

"And now, Charity Bryan, you shall pay for what you have said, and for this!" He thrust the wounded hand forward. Blood splattered against her face and she felt faint.

The stocky guard glanced at his partner, then at Granger.

"What's going on here? What are you about to do, Mr. Granger?"

Granger knelt and picked up the broken bottle neck, never taking his gaze off Charity's face. Flipping the neck into his other hand, he said in an icy voice:

"I'm just going to teach our lady friend that it isn't polite to insult a host—much less wound him. Just a little lesson in manners . . . hold her, men."

"No! Please, no . . ."

The taller guard looked troubled. "You're going to *cut* her? You're going to cut a lady?"

"Shut up! I pay you to obey orders, not question them!"

"I ain't going to take part in this, no matter what you pay me. I've done some bad things in my day, but I ain't never hurt no lady!"

The guard relaxed his grip, and Charity pulled free. Hesitating, the other guard let her go as well. Charity bolted through the door and into the morning light.

Granger swore. "I'll have you shot!"

The taller guard struck Granger, knocking him on

his back. The stocky guard still looked hesitant and confused, staring at his partner.

"Why did you . . ."

Granger's good hand came up, gripping a derringer. The stocky gunman scarcely had time to choke out a faint cry before the room was filled with the blast of the weapon, one bullet for each man.

The stocky guard took his in the forehead; the taller man was wounded in the chest. He fell to the floor, moaning. Within five seconds he was dead.

Granger stepped over the bodies and darted toward the open door.

The girl was running hard toward the open plains that stretched out before the house. Cursing, Granger raised his derringer and squeezed down the trigger, forgetting that he had fired both shots at his guards.

He ran to the body of the nearest man and grabbed the rifle that lay beside him. Working the lever and racing back to the open door, he raised the rifle to his shoulder and searched across the sight for the fleeing girl.

Suddenly he dropped the muzzle of the weapon and stared at something materializing on the horizon. Riders were approaching, moving at a steady pace toward the ranch. They were too far away for him to clearly tell who they were, but they could be bringing nothing but trouble.

Charity was forgotten now. Granger stood in silence, watching the approaching riders. As they drew nearer, he moved to a table across the room and picked up a collapsible spyglass. Returning to the door, he adjusted the instrument against his eye.

For a moment he stared through it, then quickly lowered it. He shook his head slowly. Among the riders he had seen Duke Bryan. And with him several of the other area ranchers.

Picking up the rifle once more, he darted out of the house toward the bunkhouse. Out of the corner of his eye he saw the fleeing form of Charity Bryan heading toward the approaching riders.

Still far away from the ranch house, Duke Bryan pulled his horse to a stop.

"Frank . . . is that Charity I see running toward us?"

The young man gazed intently at the feminine figure running hard toward them. Incredible though it was, his father was right. It was Charity.

"How did she get here? And where is Tucker?"

Charity was closer now. Nudging his horse forward, Frank rode out to meet her, followed by Duke.

Duke descended from his saddle and stepped forward, opening his arms to embrace his daughter. Weeping, scared, Charity collapsed into his grasp as the other riders gathered around.

"He tried to cut me, Pa . . . he tried to cut me with a broken bottle." Charity talked in a rush. "I know I shouldn't have come here, but I wanted to try to talk him out of bothering you anymore. I fooled Tucker to get him to leave me so I could come here. It wasn't his fault, so please don't blame him, Pa. I had to try to stop it from coming to a fight. I'm sorry . . ."

Duke embraced his daughter again, angry because of the dangerous move she had made, yet touched that she would so endanger herself for him. He resisted the urge to scold her, instead drawing her close and declaring his love for her. Suddenly he pulled away from her, looking into her face.

"You say he tried to *cut* you?"

Trembling, Charity could only nod.

Duke turned and looked toward the ranch house. Men were coming out of the bunkhouse and mounting horses from the nearby stable. He shook his head.

"Frank, take Charity and head back toward Buck's ranch. It looks like there's going to be a battle here."

Buck was looking at the gunmen mounting up at the

corral. "There's a lot of 'em, Duke. We just might get the worst end of this. deal."

Duke wheeled about and looked at the hefty man. "He tried to cut my daughter, Buck. I'm going to find Dan Granger and square things up with him, even if I have to go alone."

"Don't worry, Duke. You ain't going alone. But we'd best get a move on."

Duke gave a cold smile. "I'm ready, Buck."

Chapter 13

Charity and Frank scarcely made it off the scene before the shooting began. Charity's horse was still stabled at the Granger ranch, so she had no choice but to ride behind Frank on his mount.

The extra weight slowed the animal, and Frank worried that they might be overtaken by any of Granger's men that might get past the line of ranchers. Digging his heels into the flanks of the animal, Frank hoped the ranchers would be successful in putting a dent in Granger's forces.

The ranchers moved out of the open just as the shots began, toward the grove of cottonwoods along a narrow stream to their right. Granger's riders bore down on them like an advancing military line, their rifles blazing.

Duke recognized among them Thrasher and some of the others who had raided and burned his ranch the day before. It was likely that Thrasher was plenty mad right now, having his own tactics turned against him. Sliding from his saddle as soon as he had ridden into the relative safety of the trees, Duke levered a slug into his rifle chamber and squeezed off a quick shot at the hefty Thrasher.

The ranchers had lost the element of surprise when they were spotted from the ranch, and the unexpected appearance of Charity had lost them time. Duke was surprised at the number of men Granger had. He had expected that the losses in the previous raid on his ranch would have reduced the size of Granger's force considerably; instead, it appeared that the handful who had attacked the ranch were only a portion of those Granger had at his disposal. Duke wondered if counterattacking Granger on his own ground was wise after all.

No matter now. It was done, and all they could do was keep shooting from the cover of the trees, hoping they could pick off enough of the rapidly moving targets to keep from being overrun. Lifting his rifle to his shoulder, Duke squinted his left eye and bore down upon one of the riders. Squeezing the trigger with as much of a steady grip as the situation would allow, he dropped the man from his saddle. Beside Duke, Buck fired his own weapon—another rider dropped to the dirt.

Shocked by the accuracy of the ranchers' shooting, Granger's men fell back, making a wide circle, heads held low to avoid making a clear target. Duke took advantage of the retreat to place some careful shots at the fleeing men.

Dan Granger viewed the battle across the distance from the safety of the bunkhouse. He had fled there at the first sight of the approaching band of ranchers and had stirred his sleeping men awake, sending them out blurry-eyed to fight while he cowered in the safety of the thick-walled bunkhouse, watching the fight through an open window.

He had sent all of his men out to fight the ranchers—or so he thought. Unknown to him, the slim, dark figure of the gunfighter Mick Brandon was slipping quietly into the rear of the ranch house, intent on solving a mystery that had only minutes before presented itself as he made an early-morning stroll around the ranch.

Brandon had risen earlier than the other men not because it was his usual habit, but because some vague something had kept him from sleeping. Slipping on his boots, he had strapped on his gun belt and walked out into the morning, moving toward the rear of the ranch clearing for a smoke and a breath of morning air.

The mystery he was determined to solve involved two shots he had heard—thin, cracking shots like those a derringer might make. The strange thing was that they had come from the interior of the house.

It seemed likely it was Granger who had fired, for no one but him occupied the huge dwelling. And no one else would be awake except the pair guarding the place—Bill French and Mick Brandon's brother, Lester. But neither of them carried a derringer.

Brandon knew the house was now empty, for he had seen Granger slip toward the bunkhouse when the band of riders appeared on the horizon. Brandon wasn't concerned with the approaching group; he didn't care what happened to Granger, the ranch, the ranchers, or anyone else except himself and his brother. Brandon was a soldier of fortune; the right cause was the one that paid the most money. If Granger died, it wouldn't bother him in the least; there was always work for a man who was indiscriminate with his gun.

And so when Brandon saw the other men pouring out of the bunkhouse toward the stable, he made no effort to join them. He was in no mood for a battle this morning. In the confusion of the fight Granger would never know he had stayed behind, and even if he found out, the worst he could do would be to send Brandon on his way, if he had the guts. And in that case he would just hire out his gun elsewhere. He was about ready to move on anyway.

But those two mysterious derringer shots still interested him. So, slipping quietly to the back door of the log building, Brandon put his hand to the latch and pushed his way in.

He had to blink a couple of times to adjust to the darkness of the back room. He had set foot in Granger's home only once before—the time he was hired. Granger was funny about his house, Brandon knew, letting others in only occasionally, women almost never. Strange how Granger hated women. He had been jilted once when he was young, the story said, and since that time had hardly spent two minutes with any female. That seemed mighty ridiculous to Brandon, who in all his days had never felt anything resembling love, unless it was the attachment he felt to his brother.

Brandon looked around the back room. Nothing there. He moved toward the door and entered the narrow hallway leading to the main room.

The sight of the two bodies on the floor struck him like a hammer blow. It wasn't that the sight of death upset him, for he had looked on it many times after inflicting it himself, and it had never bothered him. In fact, he sort of liked it.

But the dead men on the floor were not just some strangers, like the men he had killed for money.

Bill French lay with his mouth open and his forehead plugged with a neat hole. Brandon didn't care about him—he had never liked the stocky, effeminate-voiced man anyway. But the other man was Lester, his brother.

Brandon's face grew red. Lester . . . the only member of his family whom he had cared two cents' worth about, lay dead in his own blood on Granger's floor.

Frank slowed the horse down as soon as he and Charity were far away from the battle that now sounded like no more than firecrackers popping at a distant July Fourth celebration.

Strangely, he had little to say to his sister. He felt as if he could be angry at her for doing something so foolish as walking right into Granger's ranch, but there seemed little point to anger now.

Charity felt the same way. She was happy to be alive, glad she had escaped Granger, but still things seemed no better than before. Pa was back there, facing a band of killers, shooting it out in spite of her futile attempt to keep things peaceful.

"They burned the ranch, Charity," Frank said in a dull voice.

"What?"

"They burned the ranch. Nearly killed me and Pa

and Jack, and would have if Buck and the others hadn't showed up and run 'em off. The house was burned before sundown."

They rode on farther, still saying little. Sometime later Frank saw a distant figure approaching on horseback; after a moment he recognized him.

"Yonder comes Tucker—see him?"

Charity looked over her brother's shoulder. He was right—it was Tucker. Charity's face grew red. She wondered how Tucker would react to her. Though she still believed she had only done what was her duty, she felt guilty about it at the same time. Likely Tucker had gone back to the line camp, found her gone, and worried over it.

"Howdy, Tucker. Good to see you still in one piece."

"You, too, Frank. I figured when I saw the ranch that you were killed." Tucker was talking to Frank but staring at Charity, who couldn't return his gaze with any steadiness. "Charity . . . what are you doing here? I thought you were supposed to stay at the line camp."

Frank said, "We'll fill you in later, Tucker. Right now I got to get Charity to the Treadway ranch and head on back to Granger's. Pa and Jack are there, along with some of the other ranchers, and they're fighting it out with Granger's men. They're outnumbered, too, and I plan to get back there as quick as I get Charity to Buck's place."

"Fighting . . . well, I ain't surprised. I'm heading for the Granger spread myself. I asked a sodbuster how to get there."

"All right, then. I'll see you soon."

They separated, Tucker riding faster now, his brow beaded with sweat. Riding into battle—it was something he never dreamed he would be doing.

Charity twisted her head to look at Tucker's diminishing form as they rode toward the Treadway ranch. She watched him as long as he was visible, then turned forward again, deep in thought.

Tucker listened to the rushing wind as he rode, trying to pick out the sound of gunfire. He wasn't certain if he was going in the exact direction toward the Granger spread, but he was following the directions given him by the sodbuster, and he had seen Frank and Charity approach from this direction, so he figured he was right.

But according to what he was told, he should be getting close by now. But if he was close, then why didn't he hear gunfire?

Tucker saw it then—the huge, sprawling ranch with its big ranch house and hulking bunkhouse, the grove of cottonwoods several hundred yards in front of it and slightly to the right. And he saw also, as he pulled his horse to a stop, that the battle had been a short one.

Men were congregated around the bunkhouse, standing in a rough circle. Though the distance was great, he saw some men with their hands tied behind their backs.

Tucker was at a loss. There was certainly no way he could hope to free the men single-handed, and there was nowhere to turn for aid. He seemed doomed to watch Granger do what he pleased to the captured men.

Realizing that his position was not good and that he could easily be seen from the ranch if anyone glanced his way, Tucker spurred his mount toward the cottonwoods, hoping to conceal himself there and obtain a clearer view of the ranch. But even then, what good would that do Jack and Duke and the others?

Tucker refused to consider the thought that Jack might not be among the prisoners, that he might be dead somewhere on the ranch grounds.

Tucker slipped quietly into the trees, dismounting as he entered. Tethering his horse to a branch, he slipped quietly toward the stream that ran through the grove.

His eyes fell on something in the leaves, something he couldn't immediately identify. He jumped, conscious of how edgy he was right now. He looked again. It was a brown hat, the brim ripped by what apparently had been a bullet. A brown hat . . .

Just like the one Jack wore.

"Jack?"

No answer, only the whisper of the breeze in the cottonwoods.

"Jack, are you here?"

Tucker stepped forward, treading on something soft, something other than the moist earth that lined the stream.

It was a hand.

"Jack!" Tucker cried out loudly, forgetting the danger of it.

He pushed aside the bushes that covered the face of the figure. Staring into the face of a dead man, he felt a mixture of revulsion and relief.

The man had been struck by a rifle bullet, messing up his features considerably. But it wasn't Jack. Probably one of the ranchers.

He moved on past the body, crouching in the leaves. Parting the branches just enough to let him see, he looked across the distance at the ranch house.

The men gathered there seemed to be arguing among themselves. Occasionally someone would shove one of the men standing with his hands bound, as if somehow punctuating a point by the action.

Tucker tried to make out the faces of the men. As he squinted and forced his eyes to accommodate to the distance, he made out the face of Duke Bryan among the bound men. Others he didn't recognize. But Jack . . . where was Jack?

There. He saw him, there not far from Duke, occasionally blocked from view as Duke moved about. Jack's hands were bound just like the others, but at least he was alive.

"Don't move a muscle, boy. Don't even twitch."

For a moment Tucker thought the voice had only been his imagination. But then he felt the cold touch of a .44 against the back of his neck and knew it was real.

Chapter 14

As he was led up the road toward the house with a gun pressed to his back, Tucker could tell from the somber expressions of the prisoners that they anticipated no mercy. Dan Granger stood gloating over the scene. Tucker identified him by his imperial bearing.

"I found this one down in the grove," said Tucker's captor. "I figured you'd want him, Mr. Granger."

"That I do. Who are you, boy?"

Tucker looked at Granger with contempt.

The rancher laughed. "Tough one, are you? It doesn't matter. It'll all be over soon enough anyway."

"Sorry they got you, Tucker. I reckon we won't make it back to the Crazy Woman after all," Jack said. It was evident both from his words and bearing that he had abandoned hope.

Granger walked over to Duke Bryan, a smug smile on his face. "You wouldn't yield, would you? You just wouldn't give up. And now I've got you."

He swept his glance over the others. "You didn't even have to be involved in this. But you made your choice and you'll take the consequences. All I really wanted was to deal with my dear friend, Duke Bryan. That's all."

"Why, Granger? Why do you hate me so?"

Granger said nothing, but his gloating smile faded. For a moment hatred gleamed in his eyes, then he turned away.

"Hang 'em."

Some of the gunmen guarding the prisoners looked

at each other, slightly unsure if they had heard rightly. Thrasher voiced the question.

"What did you say, Mr. Granger?"

"Are you deaf? I said hang 'em. The stable rafters will do just fine."

Tucker sensed a mounting tension among the gunmen. It hung in the air like static, a kind of vague dissatisfaction that could be perceived in the faces and eyes of the men.

Granger's eyes snapped as he looked around the group. "What are you waiting for? I told you to hang them, and I want it done now!"

Nervous glances, the sound of someone clearing his throat, uncomfortable fidgeting.

"No."

Tucker wasn't sure who the speaker was, but the quiet monosyllable caused Granger to jerk around, glaring at the group of men. Faces dropped; eyes focused on boot tops.

"Who said that?"

No answer came back, and Granger repeated the question in a tone like a patient father chiding a stubborn child.

"I asked who said that."

"I did, Mr. Granger. I ain't gonna take part in no hanging," said a blond man. "I don't know about anybody else, but ever since we tried to take this here fellow"—he gestured toward Duke—"all I've seen is trouble and folks getting shot. It seems to me that hanging these folks will get us all hanged ourselves sooner or later. It ain't worth it for what you're paying us."

The man spoke quickly, in a trembling voice. Granger stared at him as if he were an oddity.

"Are you refusing to obey an order?"

The man appeared somewhat intimidated by Granger's domineering manner, but also defiant. "Yes, sir. I am."

Granger looked at the rest of the group, studying

faces. "Is anyone else inclined to go along with Hank here?"

There was a pause. Granger slowly began to smile. His men were still under his control; his will still ruled.

That illusion was shattered by a quiet voice that spoke up, followed by others, the courage of the defiant ones growing as their numbers increased.

"Yes, sir, I'll go along with him."

"And me."

"And me. I don't want to hang."

"That's right. It's one thing to shoot a man from cover, where nobody knows who done it, but it's another to hang a man right on your own place where everybody will know it's you."

Granger sputtered, tried to speak, and failed. And in the defiance of the men Tucker found a new trace of hope.

"I don't know about these yaller devils, but I'm with you, Mr. Granger. I'm with you all the way."

The speaker was Thrasher. Granger turned to smile briefly at him, and the burly man grinned like a child who had pleased his father.

Thrasher's words drew similar responses from some of the other men. In a matter of moments the men were divided among themselves, one side ready to leave, the other ready to do whatever Granger ordered.

The rancher walked up to the man who had first defied him and thrust his face inches from the man's nose. Steely-eyed, he raised his arm and pointed to the distant horizon.

"Get out of here, the lot of you. And if I ever see you again, you'll die. Get out of here—out of the territory if you know what's good for you."

"That suits me, Granger. I been ready to cut out for weeks now anyway."

The men turned and strode to their horses, a few of them heading for the bunkhouse. Granger stopped them.

"Forget the bunkhouse. I said for you to get out of here."

"But I got—"

"*Move!*"

The men glared in anger but made no further move toward the bunkhouse. They joined those already in the saddle, and the lot of them moved off at a run, putting as much distance as they could between themselves and the ranch in as short a time as possible.

Thrasher watched them depart. "I would have been glad to have shot 'em for you, Mr. Granger."

"Shut up. Don't you see that there's only a handful of us left?"

It was true. There were only six men left guarding the ranchers—fewer guards than prisoners. But with the prisoners' hands bound and all the weapons in the possession of Granger's loyal remnant, the advantage of greater numbers was of little consequence.

"Well, men, we got a hanging to take care of," said Granger, slapping his palms together. "Take them to the stable."

Tucker felt the cold nudge of a Winchester muzzle against his back, shoving him forward. Reluctantly he moved, the gunmen steering him and his partners toward the stable on the other side of the clearing.

Granger was gleeful as he walked toward the stable. Duke Bryan would not look at him, concentrating his gaze straight ahead, refusing to hurry in spite of the nudging and goading of the men leading him.

The stable was dark and smelled of hay and horse manure. Granger stared up toward the massive rafters that arched across the top of the building. Finding the one he thought best located for the hanging, he ordered a rope thrown across it.

Granger tied the knot himself, pulling it tight and leaving it to dangle. Granger's men pulled a wagon up beneath the rope, adjusted the noose, and tied off the other end. Hitching a mule to the wagon tongue, they looked to Granger for further directions.

"We'll take 'em one at a time," the rancher said. "And though I'm tempted to save the best for last, I think we'll start with my friend Bryan."

Duke was hustled up onto the wagon. Granger stood to the side, grinning broadly at Duke, who stood almost proudly at the end of the wagon, ready to take his fate without a whimper.

"Put the rope around his neck. Bryan, I guess this is good-bye."

Duke cleared his throat and spit directly toward the arrogant rancher, the matter striking him squarely in the face. Then Duke threw back his head and laughed uproariously.

Granger swore and wiped his face on his sleeve.

"Do it! Hang him! *Hang him now!*"

"Hold it right there . . . drop the guns."

Granger whirled, along with the others, to see who had just entered the stable door, guns drawn. Though the sunlight outside silhouetted the two figures, Jack blinked and looked closely, then his mouth dropped open.

"Thurston Russell!"

The burly, red-bearded man moved around into the shadow and out of the glare of the light. He was a large man, red-faced, balding, but with a thick beard. Over his left ear was a leather patch held in place by a strap that ran across his brow and around his head.

"Well, Jack—I figured I would find you in here. I've been keeping a close watch on you the last few days. You ain't been nowhere but I knew about it. And I figured from the looks of what was going on around here that if I didn't come and get you now, I would never get my chance."

Granger stepped forward. "Who is this—"

"Shut up. And the rest of you drop them guns like I told you. That means you, too, fat boy." He waved his pistol at Thrasher. Thrasher reluctantly dropped the weapon he was fingering.

"What do you want?" Granger asked, more polite this time.

"The question is 'who,' feller. I want my old friend Jack, here. We got some old problems to settle, don't we, boy?"

"I don't figure it that way," Jack said.

Russell glanced at the noose around Duke's neck. "It don't look like you have a good choice of options right now."

Jack nodded. "You got a point."

"Then come on. I'll leave the rest of you to continue what you started."

Russell and his partner, a fellow Tucker recognized as one of the Crazy Woman's resident no-goods, hustled Jack outside at gunpoint. Russell waved his pistol in the direction of the stable occupants, making it clear that sudden moves would not be wise.

For a moment there was only silence in the stable, then everyone became suddenly conscious that the guns were on the floor, available to whoever could get their hands on them. Of course, that was a problem for the prisoners, with their hands bound behind them, but Tucker decided to try to free himself, for his bonds felt loose. With a sudden wrenching motion he yanked his hands free of their restraints.

The stable became a sudden flurry of movement, with the prisoners suddenly butting into their captors, knocking them aside. Only Duke, with the rope tight around his neck, was unable to move.

Buck Treadway sent his bulky form flying into Granger, sending him sprawling in the straw and manure. Then the rancher was a whirlwind, moving in all directions, sending bodies flying as he barreled into them.

Tucker's hand found a pistol. Not even having time

to see if it was loaded, he stood and brandished the weapon.

"Hold it!"

The fighting continued. Tucker raised the weapon above his head and fired. The reverberation echoed through the stable, deafening in the enclosed building. The fighting ceased suddenly.

"Granger—back off. The rest of you, too."

The guards moved back, inching toward the rear wall. Out of the corner of his eye Tucker saw a hand inching toward a pitchfork; as the fork was suddenly thrown full-force at him, he ducked, firing at the same time.

The man gripped his chest and fell backward, just as another of the guards leaped for a fallen weapon. He never made it. Tucker's shot struck him full in the side, knocking him off his feet before he fell dead to the stable floor.

There were no further moves. Tucker noticed a knife in the belt of Thrasher.

"Toss that knife over in this corner—hilt first."

Thrasher complied. Tucker edged over and picked the knife up, motioning for Buck Treadway to come to him. The man obeyed, and Tucker cut his bonds. Immediately Treadway picked up a rifle, then headed for the wagon where Duke stood, his neck in the noose.

Whether it was a deliberate action of one of the guards or whether the mule just spooked, Tucker never knew. But for some reason the animal decided to move forward.

Duke tried unsuccessfully to keep his footing on the moving wagon, but he became unbalanced and fell forward. Buck Treadway yelled, dropping his weapons and moving toward Duke with a speed that was incongruous for such a big man.

He caught Duke around the legs, saving him by a fraction of an inch from having his neck snapped by the jerk of the rope. But after he had hold of him, there was nothing he could do but stand there, supporting Duke's weight to keep the rope slack.

Tucker moved forward, scooping up the knife and leaping into the wagon. Keeping his pistol trained on Granger and his remaining men, he slashed the rope above Duke's head, and Treadway let his friend ease to the ground. Another slash of the knife and Duke's hands were free.

Duke and Treadway picked up weapons and took over the duty of guarding Granger and his men while Tucker freed the hands of the other ranchers.

Duke looked squarely at Granger. "It looks like your party was spoiled. Where's your army now?"

Chapter 15

Jack couldn't decide if the arrival of Thurston Russell was good or bad for him. It had saved him from the hangman's noose, but it didn't seem likely that what Russell had in store for him would be better. The big, red-bearded man was riding along directly behind him, and Jack could feel the rifle aimed at his back.

They rode eastward, putting distance between themselves and the ranch at a furious rate. And though he was concerned for his own welfare, Jack was also anxious about Tucker. By now his younger brother might be dead, swinging from a stable rafter.

The three men rode until they reached an area where a low hill dipped into a shallow valley filled with occasional rough boulders and scrubby brush.

"That's far enough. We can take care of our business right here. Are you surprised to see me, Jack?"

"No. Tucker said he thought he was followed. I figured it was you."

"That's right. I knew ol' Danver was dying, and would want to see his boy before he kicked over. He won't get that chance. And from the looks of things back there at that ranch, I don't believe Tucker will make it back home either."

Jack had nothing to say to that. He watched Russell dismount, the grin still on his face.

"Let me ask you something," Jack said. "Was it you that shot the old fellow a couple of nights back at the little ranch that got burned down?"

Russell shrugged. "I reckon it won't hurt to tell you,

since you won't be spreading any stories after I get through with you. Yeah . . . it was me. But the man shot at me first. He had it coming. You can't condemn a man for defending himself."

Jack said, "What do you plan to do with me?"

"Just a little evening up of the score," Russell said. "I've carried around the memory of you for seven years—and it comes back every time I look in the mirror and see this." He gestured toward his damaged ear and the leather patch that covered it.

"I'm sorry about that. I didn't want to hurt you, but you jumped me that night. And like you say, a man has a right to defend himself."

"And he has a right to revenge if he wants it," Russell snapped. "Down off that horse."

Jack complied, forcing himself to move slowly. He didn't want to lost his calm; a quick move might be fatal. His mind worked furiously. He knew Russell was a dull-witted and proud fellow. If there was only some way to turn that against him . . .

"Jack, you know Tater Blevins, here," Russell said, indicating the silent partner that rode with him. "Tater's agreed to help me out. We figure that the old eye for an eye principle holds true right now. Tater, you hold him, and we'll see if he likes losing an ear any better than I did."

Jack's expression didn't change. He spoke in the same calm voice as before. "Tater, you come near me and I'll thrash you. I'm warning you."

Tater glanced nervously at Russell, a bit unnerved. Russell appeared irritated at the hesitation.

"Don't worry about him, Tater—I got a gun on him."

"But what if . . ."

"I said don't worry about him. He won't hurt you. He's too scared."

Jack laughed. "It don't look like I'm the one that's

scared, Thurston. You're the one holding the gun on an unarmed man, afraid to come within ten feet of him."

"You shut up—"

"No. I might as well speak my mind, since I got nothing to lose. You've always been as big a coward as they come, Thurston. You were scared the night I cut your ear, and you're scared now. Big, brave Thurston Russell! Afraid to take me on man to man—got to have some fool to hold me so you can slice on me without worrying about it."

"I ain't afraid of nobody."

"Then fight me—no knives, no guns—just man to man. And if you can whip me, why, I'll cut my own ear off! Sound fair enough?"

Russell looked scared. Jack could read his thoughts. Russell didn't want to have to take a personal risk to get his revenge, but he also didn't want to look like a coward.

Jack smiled deliberately. "I figured as much—too scared. Tell me, Thurston—will you feel like you've had your revenge, knowing that you were scared to face me one on one? You'll kill me, sure, but will that give you satisfaction when down inside you know you're a sniveling coward?"

Russell jerked up straight. "That does it, boy! Tater, back off. Hold the gun on him if you have to, but don't fire unless you get the order from me. Understand?"

Tater nodded, slipping his .44 from its holster. Russell moved forward, slapping his fist into his palm, trying to hide his trembling. Jack dusted his hands on his thighs and smiled, unnervingly calm.

"Come on, Thurston, come and get me! I've tried for seven years to avoid trouble with you, but it hasn't done any good. Come and get me!"

Thurston roared like a bull and lunged forward, grappling for Jack's neck. The agile younger man skipped to the side, laughing as Russell stumbled past him. As he passed, Jack sent forth a wide-swinging kick that landed on the seat of Russell's pants.

"Missed me, jackass! Try again!"

Russell came back quicker than Jack had expected, managing to get a grip on Jack's shirt. He pulled the slim, younger man to him, wrapping bearlike arms around him and beginning to squeeze. Jack felt his ribs bending beneath the force, threatening to snap.

With his arms pinned to his sides, he did the only thing possible—he snapped his head forward and clamped his teeth down on Russell's nose.

The balding man cried out and released Jack. Jack stumbled backward, inhaling refreshing air into his strained lungs, but also managing to gasp out a taunt at the man who was rubbing his nose vigorously.

"You'd . . . best not try that again," he said. "You look ugly enough with just one ear. You'd look worse without a nose."

"You want me to shoot him, Thurston?" called out Tater.

"No! Leave him to me!"

Russell moved forward, arms flailing wildly. He managed to connect a solid right to Jack's jaw, knocking him to his side on the earth. Bellowing like an enraged buffalo, he threw himself in the air and fell straight toward the downed younger man.

Jack's knee came up and caught Russell in the stomach as he fell, sending his breath rushing out in a great foul-smelling burst. Before the man could recover, Jack shoved him aside and rolled over, rising to his feet.

Russell stood up, but Jack planted a hard kick against his thigh, making his leg collapse beneath him. Then he moved forward, raining punches into the fleshy face, blackening the heavily browed eyes.

Russell struck Jack hard in the belly. Jack stumbled, falling back.

Russell was on top of him, pounding him about the kidneys. Jack felt consciousness begin to slip away.

"How . . . does it . . . feel, boy?" gasped Russell. "How do you . . . like it?"

Jack wasn't sure just what he did next; he simply let his body explode into movement. But whatever he did, it worked, for Russell gasped and rolled back off him.

Jack managed to rise, still dazed and throbbing with pain. But now wasn't the time to quit; he stumbled forward, punching Russell hard in the left kidney.

Tater stood to the side, watching it all with great concentration, not paying attention to anything around him except the battle on the grass. And so he was taken completely by surprise when he felt the cold barrel of a Winchester nudge his left ear.

"Drop the gun."

The speaker was Tucker. He had approached unnoticed, along with Duke and a handful of the other ranchers. Taking Tater's weapon, he looked down at the combatants.

"Should we break 'em up?" asked Duke.

Tucker frowned, then shook his head. "No. This is something that has been festering for seven years. It's time they had it out and ended this once and for all."

Duke shrugged. "Whatever you say. He's your brother."

Russell had Jack around the neck right now, doing his best to choke him. But Jack was pouring a steady series of blows to Russell's stomach and kidneys, every one weakening the big man a little further. Gradually the grip on Jack's neck lessened, then let go.

Jack moved in then, still pounding Russell's gut, giving an occasional uppercut to the chin. There was no sound in the little valley other than the grunts and moans of the two men and the sound of fists slapping flesh.

Russell did his best to rally, trying to return the blows he was receiving, but the agile Jack managed to deflect most, still relentlessly letting the big man have it on the gut. Russell's face was fiery red, and his cheeks puffed out with each blow to his stomach. When Jack saw the man's eyes roll up in his head and his mouth drop open, he knew it was over. He sent a final punch into the man's face, and Russell dropped straight back, moaning and drifting in and out of consciousness.

Jack knelt beside him and lifted his head up by the shirt collar. "Listen, Thurston, from now on this war is over—understand? You won't ever bother me or any of my kin again, no matter what. If you do, you'll get worse than what you got today. And don't ever think you can take me on with a gun, 'cause I can whip you that way just as good as I can with my fists. Now I'm going to let you get up from here and ride away, because I don't want to hurt you—I never did, even when I cut your ear. The trouble is over—I'll never run from you again, and you'll never chase me. Understand?"

Bleary-eyed, breathless, filled with pain, Russell could only manage to grunt out an assent. Jack let Russell's head drop back to the dirt, then he stood and noticed for the first time the band of men watching him on the hill. When he saw Tucker among them, his hard-pounding heart leaped within him.

"Tucker! Lord, boy, I thought you would be dead!"

Tucker headed down the slope toward his brother. "Not quite, Jack. I was worried the same for you."

Jack snorted. Glancing down the slope to where Russell was picking himself up from the dirt, he said, "I don't think I'll have anything to worry about from Thurston anymore. I think he'll leave all of us alone from now on. I'm going back home, Tucker. Ma will be needing us both if Pa dies. I ain't running no more."

"I'm glad to hear it, Jack."

"But how did you get away from Granger? And where is he now?"

Tucker walked back up the slope toward the waiting men, his hand on his brother's shoulder. "Granger's our prisoner now, Jack. We managed to overpower them in the stable. Duke and me and the others came after you, worrying about what Russell might do. It looks like we didn't have anything to worry about."

"What have you done with Granger?"

"Buck is taking him back to his ranch, along with the men left with him."

Jack shook hands with Duke. "Well, I figure the worst of it is probably over."

Duke smiled weakly. "I hope so. But we got a problem, still. And that's what we're going to do with Granger."

"We could turn him over to the law . . . well, I guess not the law around here. Granger runs that."

"He sure does. And what kind of proof do we have against him that would stand up in court? We're stuck with a prisoner and nothing to do with him."

"I see the problem. Maybe if we head on to Treadway's ranch we can figure out something once we all get there."

The men mounted up, first seeing off Thurston Russell and his partner. The one-eared man looked like an injured child, his pride completely shattered, cowardice replacing what spirit he had possessed before. He headed due south, probably going back to the Crazy Woman, Jack figured. And although fighting it out with his adversary had lifted a burden from Jack's mind, still he wondered what would happen when their paths inevitably crossed again.

The men started westward toward the ranch.

Spirits were low in spite of the victories of the last hours. Several ranchers had been killed in the battle at the Granger ranch, and breaking the news to the waiting families would not be easy. There would be several bodies to gather and burial services to be held.

The day was almost gone when the men arrived at the ranch. Frank was with them now; he had met them along the way. He had already encountered Buck Treadway returning with Granger in tow, and he had received a complete report on the battle. But he was fascinated to hear about Jack's fight with Russell and made Jack repeat the story more than once, laughing at what he considered funny details. Jack couldn't figure it out; it wasn't funny to him.

Buck Treadway lived alone in the small cabin that constituted his ranch house. And it was obvious that a woman's touch was lacking in the place; empty tin cans were strewn about everywhere, the bed looked as if it were covered with the same linens it had worn five years before, and the floor had almost a half inch of dirt on it at some places. But after the traumas of the day, it was an inviting place, and Tucker entered it joyfully.

Seeing Charity was the best part. She sat in a hand-made chair beside the fireplace, staring with obvious discomfort at Dan Granger, who lay bound on the bed across the single room. When the men entered, she brightened. And Tucker couldn't help but notice that she brightened all the more when he brought up the rear of the party.

Buck Treadway greeted them all cordially, slapping Jack on the back and declaring he was glad to see him. Once more Jack had to tell the story of his bout with Thurston Russell.

Night fell, and Tucker grew restless. He walked over to Charity and quietly asked if she would be willing to take a walk with him about the ranch grounds. He was honestly surprised when she said she would.

Dan Granger watched Tucker and Charity walking out together, and he both hated and envied them. The girl was the image of her mother, and that stirred uncomfortable feelings in the man. Like Duke and his wife before them, Tucker and Charity appeared destined for the kind of human relationship Granger could never know. Granger had learned many things in his life, but giving and receiving love was not one of them.

His childhood life had been spent on gray New York streets, back alleys, and in dimly lit tenements. Strange thing, memory; though in his youth he never really saw his surroundings sharply, never found anything amid the unfocused drabness to stand out from the rest, yet all these years later he saw it all vividly.

In particular, the often-uplifted hand of the man he had called his father. But he was a father only in a manner of speaking and gave nothing to his secondhand son except the last name of Granger and scars on his mind and body that had never faded.

Granger remembered his father's grimacing face glaring down as he beat his stepson. He remembered the throb of every blow through him and the unending ache that remained like the wake left by a ship. He heard the curses, the abusive talk, and remembered pleading for help from his mother and that she never gave it.

Granger's mother had been a prostitute, practicing her profession openly before her son, for she had lost shame early on. Granger had received a blatant and gritty understanding of human relations at base level by simple observation. He gained two things from that: hatred of his mother and a simultaneous longing for and loathing of women in general. Throughout his life he had never overcome that. His relationships with females were from his earliest days mere encounters that lasted as long as it took to force himself physically upon them. He had narrowly escaped prosecution on rape charges three times, once only by bribing his way out. That itself would have been impossible except for Granger's closest thing to a redeeming characteristic: he was an excellent businessman.

Granger's first business venture, financed by stolen money, was a partnership in a slaughterhouse. From there he followed a basically backward route into the cattle business, first buying into cattle farms in New England, then finally heading west as his wealth and acumen grew. His combination of streetwise ruthlessness and natural dealing skills worked well for him, eventually making him into a major Montana Territory rancher who wielded much political power and had as many gunmen as cowboys in his hire.

He had come from enclosing streets of poverty to the land of open sky and wealth. Granger thought over his pilgrimage often, and it brought him the closest thing to happiness he had ever known. If that was not a great thing, it was at least something.

He cursed beneath his breath and tried to loosen the bonds around his wrists.

Chapter 16

The prairie was a wide ocean of grass covered by a dark blanket of sky pinpointed by stars. Tucker recalled how he had felt a vague loneliness beneath the stars on the journey up from the Wyoming Territory. He felt something akin to it tonight, though not quite the same, for Charity was beside him.

They walked around the back of the house, toward the corral. So peaceful were the plains that the horrors of the day seemed unreal. Tucker stopped by the corral fence and leaned one foot upon it. Charity stood beside him, so close he could feel the warmth of her on his shoulder, tingling through him like electricity.

"It's beautiful," she whispered.

"What? The corral?"

Charity laughed. "No, silly—the sky."

Tucker blushed, feeling like a fool. He realized suddenly that Charity's opinion of him was very important. He began to wonder what she did think of him.

"Tucker . . . I'm sorry I fooled you out there at the line camp. I didn't want to get rid of you . . . I just knew you wouldn't let me go to Granger's ranch, and I felt like I had to go. It was a mistake, I can see now."

"It was," he said. "But everything turned out all right, so it don't matter. I admire you for it, really. It was a brave thing to do."

"Tucker?"

"Yeah?"

"I want to thank you for what you've done for us. You risked your life when you didn't have any real call to, you and Jack both. If not for you, my Pa would be dead right now, maybe Frank, too."

"Oh, I don't see that anything I did was that important."

"It was . . . and I admire you for it. I hope you know I'm grateful."

They didn't talk much after that but instead walked about the ranch, admiring the beauty of the wild, night-shrouded prairie and the distant hills that stood out mysterious and beckoning in the moonlight. Tucker found himself wishing that the night would go on forever with Charity beside him.

They walked farther. Tucker knew it would not be wise to range far, so he and Charity stayed within quick running distance of the ranch house, enjoying the night breeze.

An hour passed. Tucker began to consider going back to the ranch house. He knew that a continued absence from the others might worry them. Reluctantly he turned to her to suggest a return.

He looked into eyes wide with horror. Something struck his head, lightning flashed across his vision, then he was down, his mind reeling into the oblivion of senselessness.

Hands picked him up; he was dragged somewhere. He was conscious of the opening and closing of a door; vague, shadowy faces hovered above him; he lay on something soft.

When he came to at last, he was in the ranch house, on the same bed on which Granger had been tied. The rancher had been evicted from it and was sitting glumly in the opposite corner. Tucker stared up at the circle of faces hovering above him.

"Charity?"

"Gone," said Duke. His voice was cold and heavy, like lead.

"Who . . ."

"It must be Thurston Russell," said Jack. "I don't know who else it could be."

"But why would Thurston Russell want Charity? What good would she do him?"

"I don't know."

Tucker sat up in the bed, his head throbbing. Duke touched his shoulder. "Do you think you should be up?"

"I want to help look for Charity."

"You up to it?"

"I am. Nothing could keep me from it."

"Then let's go. There's some already out looking. I waited around for you to wake up."

Tucker stood, rubbing his head, shaking his pounding skull to clear the cobwebs. Blinking, staggering a little, he moved toward the door, hoping his strength would return.

Duke, Jack, and Tucker headed out into the night.

"We found you over there. You had been gone a long time; we had started worrying," Jack said, pointing to the east.

"We don't know how long you had been lying there, and we couldn't find any decent sign of anyone else to follow. But Charity was gone—there was no doubt about that," Duke said.

"Look yonder—here comes Buck and the others," said Jack.

"Do they have Charity?"

"I don't believe so."

Buck Treadway approached at the head of a group of men. His face reflected disappointment. "We couldn't find her, Duke. And whoever it was that took her covered his trail real well."

"No sign at all?" Duke's voice sounded cracked and weak, as if his nerves were near snapping.

"None, Duke. I'm sorry."

"Well, I'll just have a look for myself . . . there's got to be some sign."

"If you want, Duke. But you won't find anything tonight."

Duke closed his eyes and shook his head. Tucker noticed that he was trembling. The strain of losing his ranch house and nearly his life, then having his daughter snatched from under his nose, was too much for him.

Unexpectedly, he turned on Tucker. "Why couldn't you have protected her? Too busy thinking about something else, maybe? Just what did you have in mind to do with her?"

Tucker's mouth dropped open; he was too taken aback to speak.

Duke struck him, hard. Then he leaped upon him, pounding Tucker about the face.

Buck and Jack moved simultaneously, taking Duke by the shoulders and pulling him off his dazed victim. Duke yelled, flailing his arms and trying to break free. Then, just as suddenly, he collapsed into Buck's arms, weeping.

"Get him inside," Buck said.

They moved Duke back into the house. He was still weeping loudly, apologizing for what he had done. Granger, seated in the corner, smiled for the first time since his capture. Tucker gave him a look that caused the smile to fade immediately.

Tucker sat at the table across from Duke. Duke raised his head and looked at the young man through bleary eyes. "I'm sorry, Tucker. I didn't mean what I said, and I didn't mean to jump you. It's just that when I think about Charity out there . . ."

"I understand, Duke."

A voice called from the plains, a distant voice, faint.

"I've got the girl, and I'll kill her unless you listen to me and do what I tell you."

Duke leaped up. Rushing to the door, he flung it open and stared out into the darkness. He could see no one.

"Who are you?"

"Never mind that. Yell out, sweet thing, and let them know I got you."

Charity's voice, trembling and thin, carried through from somewhere in the darkness. Duke called out to her, profoundly relieved to hear her voice, yet also frightened.

"Are you all right, Charity? Are you hurt?"

"I'm fine, Pa. But please do as he says—he means it when he says he'll kill me."

"You hear that, Bryan? She's telling the truth."

Tucker glanced over at Jack, who had a somber expression on his face. "That ain't Russell, Tucker."

"I know. But who, then?"

"I don't know. I never heard that voice before."

"We're listening," Duke called. "What is it you want?"

"I want Dan Granger."

The rancher leaped up from his chair in the corner, straining at his bonds. "No! Don't let him near me! You can't."

"Shut up, Granger," muttered Duke. Then he called out again. "What do you mean, you want Granger? Why should we turn him over to you? Who are you?"

"Never mind who I am—just do what I tell you, or the next shot you hear will be the one killing your daughter. I know you got Granger. Show him at the door."

Duke withdrew into the house. He looked at Buck Treadway and asked, "What do you think?"

"That's what I was going to ask you. I don't want to see Charity put to no harm, but I don't like giving in to a demand like that, either."

"That's Charity out there, Buck. That's my daughter."

Buck nodded. "You're right." He turned to the trembling Granger. "C'mon, mister. Show yourself at the door like he said."

The rancher pulled back, violently shaking his head. "No—you can't make me do that!"

The unidentified voice came ringing again across the distance. "I'm waiting! My patience is running out!"

Duke grabbed Granger and jerked him forward. "C'mon! C'mon or I'll shoot you dead right here!"

The cattleman struggled and fought all the way, but soon Duke held him in place in the doorway.

"Is that Granger?" the voice called.

"It's him!"

"Much obliged."

Three shots came in such rapid succession that the noise of them was like a blur of sound. Two slugs pounded into the wall, but a third clipped away some of the flesh of Granger's right leg. He collapsed. Duke pulled back inside out of instinct.

That Granger could move quickly enough to escape did not seem possible, but he did. He rose on his bleeding leg, his hands tied behind him, and bolted out the door as a fourth shot coughed out in the night and slapped another slug into the wall. The unknown man out on the range cursed loudly.

A loud feminine scream followed. Duke ran outside. Granger was nowhere to be seen. "Charity!" Duke shouted. He looked about; nothing could be seen of her.

Another scream, this one closer. Duke saw her then, running out of the night toward him.

"Pulled free," she said, coming into his arms. "Pulled free from him."

"Who is it?"

Charity was breathless. Duke could tell she had been badly scared. "Don't know. I don't know."

"Get back inside," Duke said. His arm still around her, he drew her toward the lighted open doorway. "You're all right, dear girl. You're all right now."

Out in the darkness, Dan Granger ran on a bleeding leg, struggling to free his wrists, bound behind his back. He was pursued and he knew it.

Two or three of the men in the cabin took out after

Granger but quickly gave up the chase. The fact was that they had no good plan about what to do with him anyway, so they let him go.

Not even Duke felt that Granger would be a threat again.

The gunmen who had been captured with Granger sat against the wall, looking imploringly at Duke. He walked over to them and looked them over. He drew a knife from his pocket, opened it, and cut their ropes.

"You may as well go, too," he said.

Glances flew among the ranchers. "Duke, you think we should do this?" Treadway asked.

"Why not? You think they'll give trouble now?"

Treadway gave the prisoners an up-and-down perusal, then shook his head.

"Thank you, thank you so much," Thrasher said. "We won't forget this, I promise."

"All I want you to promise is to get out of the country," Duke said.

"Yes, sir. Yes, sir," Thrasher said. He and the others left at top speed.

"Who do you think shot at Granger?" Treadway asked.

Duke shrugged. "Don't know, but whoever he is, I wish him luck."

It was clear, Duke Bryan saw, that Charity was deeply in love. She sat beside Tucker right now, and the two of them were lost in quiet conversation. It gave Duke a rather peculiar feeling. Always before he had been the one to whom his daughter turned when there were important things to say.

Treadway joined Duke. "They grow up too fast," he said.

"So they do." Duke gestured subtly toward Tucker. "But when they do, you hope they find one with the right kind of spirit and the right way of looking at things."

"What do you figure will come of this, Duke?" Treadway asked.

Duke smiled. "Before it's through, I'd say a houseful of grandchildren."

Chapter 17

Dan Granger lay in a draw, covered in sweat and trying not to breathe too loudly despite his exhaustion and the pain of his wounded leg. He had run hard from the ranch cabin with his hands still tied behind him, and it had seemed like the hot-breathed devil himself was nipping at the back of his neck. Yet when at last he had collapsed into the draw, he had found no one behind him. There he lay, panting, working at his bonds as he had secretly been doing for several hours back in the ranch house.

Almost loose now, and it was a good thing, like the fact his leg had stopped bleeding. A relatively superficial wound it apparently was; it didn't hurt nearly so bad now.

But that was only small comfort. Whoever was after him obviously was not one for scruples: he had tried to blast Granger away right in the doorway. Who could it be? The ranchers already had Granger at the time and would have no need of murder.

Granger gave a painful pull and his left wrist came free, leaving skin and blood on the rope. He rubbed the abraded skin, face twisted in pain. Then he untied the other wrist and tossed away the rope.

If not a rancher after him, then who? Granger strained to figure it out. Then a suspicion came.

Probably it was a rancher after all. Probably the whole incident had been a charade set up by the more unscrupulous of his captors to let Granger be murdered but still provide them an alibi for the law and their weaker-kneed friends. Who shot Granger? they would be asked. We don't know. Some killer out in the dark. Surely wasn't us.

Clever and heartless, those damnable ranchers. Granger glowered, still rubbing his wrists. He wouldn't stand for such. He wasn't a man to be toyed with. He had power, gunmen at his command . . .

Then he remembered. His gunmen had been routed, his power stripped, at least for the moment. Suddenly he felt even more helpless than before, and utterly alone there on the dark prairie.

Noise . . . he dropped on his face, his breath almost choking off. He nearly panicked.

How close the man passed, Granger did not know, for he never lifted his face from the dirt. But somehow, despite Granger's uncontrollably loud breathing and pounding heart, the man did pass by. After a few moments Granger knew he was alone again.

He had to get back to his ranch, figure out where he stood. He saw no real logic to it—likely there would be nothing gained by going home again—but away from his familiar refuge he couldn't even think. It was an ironic situation to feel more trapped out in the open than in enclosing walls, but that was how it stood.

He stood and immediately went down again. His leg was completely numb; the wound must be worse than he thought. But then Granger laughed to himself. He had realized it wasn't his wounded leg that had no feeling, but his good one. He had lain upon it in such a way as to cut off the circulation of blood. Now it began to tingle electrically, a million needle jabs of pain bolting through it from the inside out.

He danced clumsily about until the tingling left and feeling returned. He began walking across the prairie toward his ranch.

Like many of Granger's worst memories, it was a recollection old yet fresh: fingers wrapped too tightly around his throat, squeezing until stars exploded in his brain. "You've got the neck of a chicken, you have. I can wrap my fingers around it like it was a sapling, and snap it like a twig. Prestilent little thief! If I did kill you, who would complain? Your father? Your sow of a mother?"

The fruit seller laughed foul breath into the boy's face. His features were big and distorted by proximity, his skin gray in the shadows of the towering New York buildings on either side of the alley where the pear-stealing boy had been caught. "Light as a feather you are, Danny Granger. Toss you into the harbor and you'd float to France, eh? How light are you, anyway?"

The fruit seller lifted his young victim by the neck and held him aloft. "Hang you will someday, my little thief. Maybe by then you will have put enough meat on your bones to let you choke it out proper." He threw Dan Granger to the pitted alley floor.

The boy rubbed his neck and gasped for air. The fruit seller pointed at him and said, "You come about my stand again and you'll have my boot bruising your backside, or maybe a knift betwixt the shoulder blades."

Dan Granger's voice squeaked out, weakened because of the choking: "Someday I'll be big and strong enough that men like you will be afraid of me. Someday I'll wipe out men like you with a word."

The fruit seller laughed and turned away. Dan Granger rubbed his neck again and marked it in his mind that one day he would get his revenge.

Seven years later he raped the fruit seller's daughter.

Now, as he stumbled on his wounded leg through a grove of cottonwoods, Granger smiled at the thought. Taught that old man to treat him so, he surely had!

Granger had lost track of time as he crossed the prairie, but he felt the coming of dawn not far ahead. His house lay far before him, and he pushed on.

"You were wrong, old man—I won't hang," he said

aloud. "You were wrong and I was right: I won't hang, and I can wipe out men like you with a word."

He pushed on until he reached his ranch.

Many hours later he sat huddled in the corner of his bedroom, hands around his knees. Around him stretched his ranch, empty but for corpses and dust. Granger stared into the opposite corner as a fly buzzed in his ear. He did not swat it away.

Only now was the possibility that it was all over really beginning to strike him. His power was gone. The small ranchers had defeated him with grit and determination. The dollars Granger paid his gunmen simply hadn't been sufficient to give them purpose enough to overcome the men whose comrade Granger had terrorized.

Duke Bryan. He silently mouthed the name as if it had a bad taste. A pitiful, penny-ante rancher who had nothing—except the one lady Granger had wanted more than anything else.

She had been a fine woman, worthy of better treatment than Granger had given her, and even he knew that. But from his earliest days Granger had never known any other way with women.

Another memory from childhood arose.

Granger, kneeling, hands uplifted. Mama, I'm sorry. I saw him hurting you and grabbed the knife. I didn't know, mama. I'm sorry.

Then came brutal blows from his father, beating down upon him. Bad for business to knife a customer, boy. Ought to throw you into the street.

He remembered his mother's wiping blood from the floor when the beating was done, and he didn't know if it was that of the man he had knifed or that of himself. She was crying. He put his arms out to her but she did not respond.

The rancher snapped his head up; the memory disappeared like smoke in wind. He had heard something outside the house. Granger stood, amazed to see ruddy evening light coming in through the west-facing window, casting brown shadows from the tall cottonwood that stood outside it. He must have been half asleep.

He crept to the window and carefully looked out. Nobody there that he could see. Something banged and he started, but it was just a shutter on the loft door of the barn. Yet that wasn't what he had heard before.

He went to a gun cabinet against the wall and threw it open. Empty! Someone had cleaned it out in the midst of the day's confusion. Maybe even one of his own men. He cursed and slammed the cabinet shut; the noise echoed through the house.

He walked out of the room and onto the stair landing. He peered down but saw no one below. He walked down the stairs. Every thump of his feet on the steps sounded unnaturally loud. Granger grew winded merely descending the staircase. He realized what a toll anxiety was taking on him, and also that he had not eaten a real meal for many hours now.

He went to the dining room and found half a loaf of bread on the table. Gnawing at the dry bread, he walked uneasily through his house as if he were looking for something but not remembering what. He didn't look to see if the bodies of the men he had shot down remained where he had left them; he didn't want to see any more of death tonight.

What could he do? Was there any place for him to go? He still had money, still could buy his own justice if he wanted. So he told himself, but it didn't seem true anymore. His spirit was broken by what had happened today, and he no longer felt like the man he had been. And even Granger knew that a man who did not believe in himself any longer could gain loyalty from no other.

The noise again. It sounded like someone moving in the back of the house.

"Granger."

The rancher stumbled back against the wall. The voice had surprised him. "Who's there?" he demanded.

The speaker must have moved, for the voice now came from a slightly different location. "I've come for you, Granger."

The voice was more familiar now but still unplaced. "Who are you? What do you want?"

"I wasn't sure you would come back here, Granger. Thought you'd be smarter than that. Guess I was wrong and you're more a fool than I thought."

Granger paused. "Brandon—Mick Brandon, is that you?"

"Who do you think it is?"

"Why are you here?"

"I come to pay you the price for a dead brother. Death for death."

Granger's heart hammered. His blood raced through his veins like whitewater. "I didn't want to do it, Mick. They forced me."

"But you did do it. You . . . and so it's you who pays."

"I don't want trouble with you, Mick."

"Too late. Too late when you pulled the trigger on my brother."

Granger was backing away. He still could not see Mick Brandon even though he sensed he was drawing nearer. The house seemed very dark now.

"What do you want from me?"

"Nothing but what I was denied out there on the prairie: a good clean shot. This time I'll do a lot more than nick you."

Granger turned to his left and ran. A gunshot roared, echoing in the house. Panicked, the rancher lunged up the stairs.

He realized when he reached the landing that he had made a mistake. From here there was nowhere to go. He ran back into his bedroom for the lack of any alternative. He slammed the door and lowered the latch as if somehow that could do some good.

On the stairs the boots of Mick Brandon beat out a slow, ascending funeral-march rhythm.

"No!" Granger yelled. "Go away! Leave me alone!"

Still the boots against the stairs, then the landing.

"No!" Granger screamed again. He lurched to the window and threw it open. Out on the porch roof he climbed. The cottonwood reached up its branches toward him like the arms of a mother finally responding to a child who has reached out to her.

Granger did not miss the irony of that even as he leaped.

One kick gained Brandon entry into the bedroom. He thrust out his pistol, swept the room with it. Granger was gone. The window stood open with the curtains trailing out of it into the thickening dark.

Brandon went to the window, bent, and stuck out his head and his pistol. "Granger!" No answer. He cursed and called the name again as he pulled himself out the window and onto the roof.

He walked to the edge and looked down into the cottonwood. He lifted his pistol, then slowly lowered and leathered it. No need for a bullet now; the job was already done.

He turned his back and reentered the window, descended the stairs, left the house, and rode away. Behind him the corpse of Dan Granger bounced slightly up and down, as if hung from a spring, each time the wind moved the branches of the cottonwood. Granger's snapped neck was tightly wedged in the crotch of the largest branch, his limp body dangling below. He had, at least, died quickly.

Chapter 18

Jack and Tucker set out in the morning for the Crazy Woman. After all that had happened, it didn't seem possible, somehow, that they were at last doing what they had planned to do in the first place.

But Tucker couldn't regret having stayed and helped out the Bryans. Especially when he thought about Charity Bryan. He was sad to leave her. Jack sensed his brother's feelings as he rode beside him.

At last he ventured a question. "Missing her, Tucker?"

Tucker glanced over at Jack rather sharply, surprised by the query. For a moment he felt defensive, as if he should deny the truth. But instead, he shrugged and quietly nodded.

Jack looked ahead and grinned. "Well, if the looks of things are any indication, I'd say she's missing you, too. I could tell from the way she watched you from the beginning that she thought you were really something."

Jack and Tucker came to Pumpkin Creek and began following it down its course, heading almost due south. They rode steadily, with few breaks, and by nightfall they had come almost to the southern extremity of the creek. There they made camp.

They talked of their father, and of the difference the past seven years had made in their lives. In the bustle and danger of the recent days, Tucker had had little time to think of his father, but now that he was alone with Jack beneath the stars, with no one around to distract him, the sadness returned, and he prayed that he would find his father alive.

Jack was talkative the next day, for they were approaching familiar territory. They reached the Powder River and followed along the bank, steering east of the Hanging Woman Creek.

"I don't want to get around ol' Drake anymore. He'd probably have my tail for that stolen saddle, even though it wasn't me that took it. He's as sour as week-old buttermilk," Jack said.

They camped that night on the banks of the Powder and the following day rode until they were in the Wyoming Territory. The next day would bring them to the Crazy Woman and Danver Corrigan.

They rose early the next morning, before dawn. After eating a quick breakfast, they rode southwest along the river.

They rode all day without stopping, for the excitement of being home kept them from growing tired or hungry.

The ranch looked deserted when they approached, but a thin white trail of smoke from the chimney told them that the family was there. Tucker's heart jumped to his throat as he drew near, and Jack felt such a turmoil of emotions that he didn't know if he was happy or sad.

The door opened when they were within two hundred yards of the house. Ma stepped out into the yard, crossing her arms as she always did, watching the approaching pair. They rode up close, and only then did they see the tears in her eyes as she looked at Jack.

"Welcome home, Son," she said.

"Hello, Ma," answered Jack. "It's good to be back."

He dismounted and walked slowly toward the mother he hadn't seen in seven years. Then he took her in his arms.

"Is Pa . . ."

"He's still living," she said. "But he isn't good. It's only been the hope of seeing you come back that has kept him going."

Tucker dismounted and led the horses to the stable.

It didn't bother him that his mother had not even greeted him; he knew that the return of Jack was of such profound significance for her that all other considerations faded from her mind. After seeing to the horses, he entered the cabin and slipped quietly past the silent children to the back room.

Ma stood with her arm over Jack's shoulder, and both of them were at the bedside, looking down into Pa's face. And the best thing of all was that in spite of the tears that filled his eyes, Pa was smiling, his face radiant. Pa had aged so fast, it seemed, getting old before his time over these past seven years. But now that Jack was home, again back within these walls where he belonged, it was as if everything was right again, as it had been in the days before Jack left.

Tucker turned away. Somehow it was too much to watch. He returned to the main room of the house, where the children sat in silence, not sure just what to think about the sudden materialization of a man who for seven years had been almost mythlike in their minds. Little Tara and Benjamin Elrod were more taken aback than the others, for when Jack had left home Tara had been only a year old and Benjamin hadn't even been born.

"Is that Jack, Tucker?" Tara asked.

"Yes, honey, that's him."

"Is he here to stay?"

"I believe so, Tara."

"That's good. Pa's been hoping he would."

Jack stayed in the room with his father a long time, even after Ma came back out and joined the rest of the family. Only then did she come over to Tucker and hug him, thanking him for what he had done.

"We were worried about you, though. What slowed you down?"

"That's a long, long story, Ma. I'll wait till Jack's with me to tell it."

Jack came out of the back room at long last, a look of

contentment on his face. He came to each of the family members and greeted them, shaking the boys' hands and hugging the girls. When he met Benjamin Elrod, he didn't know what to say; he hadn't been aware he had a new little brother before Tucker told him about it.

Tucker heard Pa calling his name. He entered the rear room. Pa lay on his back, his head propped up on a feather pillow. He motioned for Tucker to come over and sit on his bedside.

"You did good, Son. I'm proud of you. Jack told me what happened. You proved yourself a man."

"Thank you, Pa."

"Of course, we don't want to tell your mother all about it."

"I understand that, Pa."

Pa let his head settle back into the softness of the pillow. He stared upward at the ceiling, looking very tired, but with a peaceful expression on his face, something calm about him that hadn't been there before.

"Seeing your brother was a dream fulfilled for me. I figure I'm still on the road to my grave, but I can go with a lot more peace now. But that's going to leave you with a lot of responsibility—Jack, too.

"Jack is going to stay, he says, and he wants to run the ranch. But you're going to have to keep an eye on him to see that he don't go to the gambling table any too often. A man can lose everything he has a lot faster than he might think."

"I know, Pa."

"Your biggest responsibility will be to look out for your ma after I'm gone, and keep an eye on Jack, at least until you leave."

"Leave, Pa?"

Danver Corrigan looked into his son's eyes. "You know you can't stay, not if you love her like I love your ma."

Tucker was surprised. Jack must have told Pa about Charity.

"I did figure on leaving to court her a little, nothing permanent, at least not yet."

"Do you love her?"

Tucker looked away from his father's intent face. "I do."

"Then it'll be permanent. That's how it's supposed to be. I'm happy for you, Son. Me and your mother—we never had nothing to amount to much as far as money was concerned, but we've had a lot of love. I wish the same for you. I wish it for all of my children and their children, too."

Tucker walked over to the window. To leave . . . to put aside his home and roam away . . . it was a peculiar thing to think about.

In the past few days he had lived not like a boy but like a man. Even Pa had said that just now.

And a man needed a mate, someone to share his life with and to love more than he loved himself.

"You're right, Pa. I will be leaving. Funny . . . I didn't know it myself."

"When do you figure you'll leave, Son?"

Tucker shook his head. "I don't know. I know I'll stay until . . ."

Danver Corrigan smiled. "Go ahead and say it . . . until I'm dead. There's no point in mincing words."

"I figure that after that I'll stay around and see that the ranch is in good order, give Jack a hand and all. Then I'll head north again."

Danver Corrigan's eyes closed, and he breathed deeply. It was obvious he was growing weary. The new burst of life Jack's return had brought him was beginning to wear off, and his face was growing gaunt and pale once more.

Tucker stood and watched him until he thought he was asleep. Then quietly he turned and started to leave the room.

"Tucker?"

"Pa?"

"There's something else I want you to do for me. Jack told me about his fight with Thurston Russell, and how he thinks the trouble is over. Maybe he's right—I hope so. But look out for Thurston Russell. He don't forget fast."

"I will, Pa. I promise."

"Good. Go on, Son. I think I'll rest a bit."

It was early the next morning that Tucker was awakened by his mother's hand, jostling him gently. He sat up in bed and looked at her weary face.

"He's gone, Tucker. He died peaceful and easy, and he died happy."

Tucker looked out through the window toward the brilliant light of the stars. The wind moaned around the eaves of the house, infinitely mournful. To Tucker it seemed a fitting farewell to the soul of Danver Corrigan.

Tucker and Jack watched the approach of the wagon bearing the simple pine coffin made of planks. The elderly man driving it pulled the mules to a halt and climbed down. He came to the young men and bobbed his head in hello.

Jack walked over and touched the coffin. "We appreciate you, Pete. You did a fine job."

"When you're old as me, you've had plenty of practice," the man said. "I've built coffins for more than I could count. Good men, bad men, men somewhere in between like most of us." He paused. "Your pa, he wasn't like most. A good man, no finer to be found." Pete slipped off his hat. "If your ma's inside, I'll pay my respects to her."

"Thanks again, Pete."

It seemed a strange and alien thing for Jack and Tucker to unload the coffin from the wagon and know it would hold their father's body. They carried it to the porch and set it there, then stood looking at it.

"I lost a lot of years with him," Jack said reflectively. "I never should have left just because of Thurston."

"You had no choice," Tucker said. His voice sounded tired.

"Yes, I did. I just didn't know it." Jack chuckled thoughtfully. "You know, Tucker, many's the time I wondered if I left to avoid trouble, or just because I was afraid. I've thought myself a coward often enough."

Tucker looked at his brother in mild surprise. "You? No. Anything but a coward."

Jack nodded. "I know that now. The trouble we had up there"—he pointed northward—"showed me that much at least."

"It showed me something else, too," Tucker said. "There's more than one way to look at success. Pa never thought he had much of it, but as far as I'm concerned, he had a heck of a lot more than Dan Granger ever did. Money, power, none of that did Granger much good that I can see."

"That's a fact. One minute a rich man with gunmen and land, the next nothing."

"You know," Tucker said, "I don't think I'll ever completely understand men like Dan Granger. I know I don't want to be like that myself."

"Amen to that, brother."

Pete the coffin maker came to the door. "Bring it in, boys," he said. "We're ready."

Tucker and Jack picked up the coffin and carried it into the house.

Danver's body lay on his bed. His eyes were closed. His whiskers had been shaved and his hair was neatly combed. He looked peaceful. The lines and gauntness left by his sickness didn't seem so evident now.

Carefully they lifted the body from the bed and placed it in the coffin. They folded Danver's arms across his chest.

Tucker looked at Jack. In his older brother's eyes tears brimmed. Jack looked down at his father's face.

"I could have been a better son," he said. "I could have stayed close by him. But somehow I never thought about the years I was losing. I never thought about him being gone."

"No regrets, Jack," Tucker said. "You can't let there be regrets."

"There's always regrets, Tucker. More for some of us than for others."

Chapter 19

Danver Corrigan was buried in a small plot beside the ranch clearing. His tomb was marked with a single wooden cross with no inscription other than his name and date of birth and death. Tucker and Jack dug the grave and stood beside it as a preacher who lived over toward the Bighorn Mountains conducted the brief and simple graveside ceremony.

Ma put up a good front, not letting herself cry except just a little, but all of the children knew that in her heart she grieved deeply for her mate. The family stood with her beside the grave for a time, then left her alone with her thoughts.

Tucker and Jack walked off together to the far end of the ranch at Tucker's request, for he needed to talk to his brother.

"Jack, I can't stay long. Me and Pa talked about it, and I know now that I'll have to be leaving soon."

"I can understand that, Tucker. But Ma needs you right now. Charity's important, but so's Ma."

"I know that. I ain't about to run off at first light or anything. It's just that . . . I don't know. I can't explain it. It's like it's eating at me or something. Ever since I talked to Pa. I know my life ain't centered here no more."

Jack shook his head. "Tucker, I've been roaming for seven years, and I'm sick of it. This ranch is home for me now, and I don't plan to leave it. I hope you can learn from my experience without trotting all over the country yourself. Stay around, Tucker. You'll be happier for it."

Tucker walked around the ranch grounds that evening and thought over what Jack had said. He found himself with conflicting impulses, pulling him in all directions.

What Jack said made sense, in a way. He knew that with Pa gone, Ma needed all of her kin close around her, especially Jack and him, who were more mature and understood her needs and feelings better than the others. He didn't want to desert Ma . . . but . . .

His father's words kept playing through his mind. Jack understood some things, but not how Tucker felt about Charity. Jack had been forced from his home and had wandered without real motive or purpose, but for Tucker it was different. He had good reason to want to head north.

But for now, he would stay here. At least until the ranch was going well and Jack had things under control.

The days passed, and Tucker did just what he knew his Pa would have wanted—he worked hard and steady, from dawn until the last light faded. Jack was with him always, working as if he was hungry for the home labor he had missed for seven years.

About dusk exactly five days after the burial of Danver Corrigan, Tucker noticed Jack slipping on his hat and heading for the door. "Where are you going, Jack?"

"Scudder's. I thought a beer would go good."

Tucker sighed. His father's warning about Jack's gambling came back to him. But he knew better than to argue with his brother.

"Hold on a minute," he said, "and I'll come with you."

The pair mounted outside and rode toward Scudder's, the night falling fast. Jack was whistling beneath his breath but saying little. Tucker recognized the symptoms of the old gambling fever.

Scudder's was a bright spot on the side of the road, an isolated structure. There were several horses hitched to the rail out in front of the building, and music from the battered old piano spilled out through the open door and was swallowed up in the night.

They pushed their way into the saloon, getting casual glances at first from the men at the bar and around the tables, then open stares as Jack was recognized. Word of his return had not spread yet, and those who knew him were surprised to see him.

Jack walked up to the bar, ignoring them. He ordered beer for himself and Tucker. Mel Scudder filled two heavy mugs until the foam spilled over the top, then shoved them toward the brothers.

"Good to see you back, Jack," he said. "Didn't expect it after all this time."

"Had to come back when I heard Pa was ailing," Jack said, draining a swallow of beer. "I figure I'll stay awhile."

A man approached the bar, a shot of whiskey in his hand. "Howdy, Jack," he said.

"Hello, Denny. How you been?"

"Fine, mighty fine. How about you? Where you been keeping yourself the past few years?"

"I been doing some punching up about Montana, different spreads," Jack said. "I figured it was time to come home."

Denny raised his shot glass to his lips and drained a small sip of the fiery liquor. "Run into Thurston Russell lately?"

Jack looked at him blankly. "No . . . I ain't seen him since I left."

Tucker looked quickly at Jack, surprised and a bit confused. But suddenly he understood what Jack was trying to do. As far as Jack was concerned, the trouble with Russell was over. Russell had been humiliated in the fight with Jack already, and Jack wasn't about to spread that humiliation any further.

Denny gave a little grunt. "Ain't seen him, huh? I heard a different tale. I hear you and Thurston had quite a ruckus a few days back, up in Montana. Ol' Tater told me about it. Said you worked Thurston over real good."

"It ain't true, Denny. I ain't seen Thurston Russell in seven years." Jack spoke in a dull monotone, casually sipping his beer.

Denny smiled, then shrugged. "Whatever you say, Jack. I guess you'll get a chance to talk about it with Thurston himself before long. He's coming here to-night."

Only Tucker caught the almost imperceptible tensing of Jack's fingers on the handle of his beer mug. His expression and voice remained unchanged.

"That right? It'll be good to see him again."

Denny frowned at that. He hadn't expected such a calm reaction from Jack, and it confused him. He mumbled something and headed back to his table.

"Jack . . . do you think we should hang around here and wait for Russell?" Tucker whispered.

"I can't run. I'm going to be living here now, maybe for the rest of my days. I'll run into Thurston somewhere or other, sooner or later, anyway. Part of the reason I came here tonight was that I figured he would show up. I got to see if this thing is really over, or if he figures on giving me more trouble."

Tucker shook his head. "Well, I don't like to think about what might happen. Russell is a crack shot."

A voice called from the opposite corner of the room. "Got a space for one more in this poker game, Jack. Interested?"

Jack turned around and looked across the room at the speaker. Tucker watched his brother's face, seeing the sudden fever, knowing the temptation that was calling to him.

Tucker could have dropped in his tracks when Jack answered after a lengthy pause, "No . . . I better skip it, Tom. I don't play no more."

Admiration shone in Tucker's eyes as he looked into

his brother's face. Jack looked back at him with a peculiar expression.

"What are you staring at?"

Tucker grinned. "Nothing." He didn't fail to catch the vague smile on Jack's face as he turned back around.

The pair were on their second set of beers when the noise of boots on the floor at the threshold caught their attention. Jack turned slowly to find himself looking straight into the cold, expressionless face of Thurston Russell.

The noise in the saloon stopped. Mel Scudder stepped back a little. A picture of a bloody fight some seven years before was running through the saloon-keeper's mind.

"Howdy, Thurston."

No answer but a cold stare.

"Buy you a beer?"

Russell turned away, walking toward a far table. Every eye in the place was upon him, and he felt it. He cast a violent glance across the men, and heads suddenly dropped back to hands of cards, and liquor glasses were quickly raised to lips.

"Mel, bring me a beer. And I'll pay for it myself," said Russell.

The barkeep hustled quickly, pouring off a beer. He carried it across the room, foam dripping off to splash on wood already stained from years of tobacco juice, muddy boots, spilled drinks, and a little blood.

Russell took the drink and began sipping it slowly, his eyes burning into the back of Jack Corrigan, who had turned his back on the big fellow and returned to sipping his beer.

Denny stood and walked over toward Russell. Speaking in a voice that all could hear, he said, "Thurston, is that a bruise I see on your jaw?"

The burly red-haired man glared up sharply at the smiling Denny. "So it is. What is it to you?"

Denny put forth a hand, palm outward, in a gesture

of mock conciliation. "Hey now, take it easy there, Thurston. No point in being snappy. I was just asking. How did you get that bruise there anyway?"

Russell's features were stony. "Ain't none of your business, Denny."

"Why, Thurston, you got no manners at all tonight! You didn't even say hello to your old friend Jack over there, and him being gone for seven years! But maybe you got good reason to not say hello."

"What's that supposed to mean?"

"Well, I heard that you two run into each other not long ago and said your hellos then. Thurston, how did you say you got that bruise?"

Russell stood, eyeball to eyeball with Denny, who stepped back a couple of feet to keep safe distance.

"Denny, you'd best shut up or I'll have to do something about it. You understand me?"

Denny spread his arms out in a gesture of innocence. "Why, Thurston, I was only trying to be nice . . ."

Russell's arm flashed out. Jack turned around in time to see Denny hit the floor, rubbing an injured jaw. Russell towered over the fallen man, looking as if he could easily squash him out with his boot like an insect.

Denny looked scared now, but also angry. He stood, backing away from Thurston Russell. Glaring, he pointed a finger at the big man's face.

"Are you afraid I'll say what everybody knows already—about how you took off after Tucker here so you could find Jack, and how when you did find him, he whipped you so good that you came crawling home? Is that what you're afraid of?"

Jack grabbed Denny's shoulder and wheeled him around. "Listen, Denny, I told you that I ain't seen Thurston Russell in seven years. Me and Thurston, we got no trouble. We're friends now. Ain't that right, Thurston?"

Russell looked confused. He stammered, unable to

gather his thoughts, then said, "Yeah . . . that's right. Friends."

Denny frowned. "But I thought . . ."

"You ought to quit thinking then, Denny," said Jack. "It puts a strain on your mind."

Abashed, Denny returned to his seat, where he glanced up occasionally at Jack, muttering something to the men around him. Jack noticed but was unconcerned. Denny wasn't worth getting upset over.

Tucker felt an admiration for his brother that he had never felt before. Jack had become almost a new person, a matured, seasoned version of the boy he used to be, with the rough edges worn off. Pa would have been proud of his eldest son.

When the brothers left Scudder's a few hours later, they found Thurston Russell outside, waiting for them. Jack walked up to the man, unafraid, making no move to threaten him.

"I . . . I 'preciate what you done in there," Russell said, his head lowered and his voice hesitant. "You're a good man, Jack Corrigan."

He turned, mounted his horse, and rode away without looking back.

Chapter 20

Jack and Tucker never again saw Thurston Russell after that. Rumors abounded about where the man had gone, but no one knew for sure.

The days passed, and the business of everyday life on the ranch began to overshadow the sorrow the family felt at the loss of Danver Corrigan. Increasingly, Tucker felt the call of the northern plains.

Summer came on full and strong, and the cattle grew fat on the plains, eating the rich green grass. Tucker and Jack spent much time there keeping an eye on their cattle, especially the expectant ones.

Tucker knew he would not be around long. Though Jack still encouraged him to stay, the ache to move on was becoming increasingly stronger, and at night he would toss restlessly and dream of travel.

Ma did well, getting on without Pa, though he knew she could daily feel the pain of his absence. It was Ma more than anything else who made him hesitate about leaving, for he didn't want to add to her loneliness. She had the rest of the family around her, and having Jack home was a delight to her, but still . . .

Tucker knew he could never replace his father, and it was pointless to try. No matter how close he stuck to Ma, he could never be what Danver Corrigan was to her. And she didn't expect him to be.

And still the words his father had said to him on the night he died went running through his mind, urging him northward.

Charity grasped one end of the log and heaved it

upward, biting her lip as she strained beneath the weight. But Buck Treadway was beside her, pushing along with her, and together they managed to hoist the log upward to where Frank and Duke could roll it into place on the rapidly growing wall. After the burden was taken from her, she whistled in relief and wiped the beads of sweat from her brow.

"Heavy, ain't it, Charity?" puffed Treadway, also sweating profusely. "Keep this up and you'll be muscled like a man."

"I hope not," she said. "I'd sure hate to look like you."

Treadway laughed and walked away.

Since they had started rebuilding the ranch house, Charity had had little time to think of anything other than hard work. But nothing was able to squeeze out of her mind the thoughts of Tucker Corrigan or the desire that he would return as he had promised.

It was funny, in a way. Just as she had realized that Tucker was much more than just another stranger whose path had crossed hers, he was taken from her. And now it seemed that she spent half of her time glancing toward the southern horizon, hoping to see him approaching.

Frank and Duke were aware of Charity's feelings. Duke approved of his daughter's interest, for Tucker had proven himself a worthy and brave man.

Duke spent many long hours mulling over the departed Dan Granger, asking aloud on many occasions if anyone had any idea why he had chosen to antagonize him so. Charity never spoke up, and she never would.

When Seth Bailey in his dying breath told her about the night he found Granger molesting her ma, it shook her to her soul, and she understood why Ma had never said anything about it. It must have been a heavy burden on the victimized lady.

Charity knew she had been right about Dan Granger. It was inconceivable to her how Granger could have lived in the way he did, locked away from humanity, his only dealings with women apparently being the violent type in which he had sought to involve her mother.

Granger was buried on the grounds of his ranch. His estate was in confusion, for he had no heirs and no living relatives anyone knew about. Many ranchers were helping themselves to any Granger cattle they ran across on the plains.

The house the Bryans were building was on the same site as the old one, but it was larger and better. Duke was in no danger because of the phony accusation of rustling or the jailbreak; the sheriff was alone now, not backed up by Granger, and he wouldn't make a move against him.

Duke had seemed ten years younger ever since he started work on the new house, and in spite of the backbreaking labor he had retained enough energy at the end of most days to make an evening trip into town for some relaxation with his friends at one of the local saloons.

The house was completed before the coming of summer. Charity was given the task of helping restock the house. Duke had included an honest-to-goodness kitchen in the new house, which excited Charity. Before, it had been only a cast-iron stove and a shelf; now she had several cabinets with swinging doors, a heavy wooden table . . . but the same old stove, which Duke had managed to salvage from the burned-out remnant of the old house.

Duke found his daughter sitting alone about dusk in early August, her skirt spread around her, her hands fingering a soft blade of grass. He approached her and sat down beside her.

"You kind of like that boy, don't you, Charity?"

She smiled, rather sadly.

Duke eased himself down into the grass, slipping his arm over his daughter's shoulder. "He's a good boy, Charity. He'll be back."

Charity looked at her father. "Will he, Pa? It's been months, and I haven't seen him. He's forgotten me, Pa."

Duke hugged his daughter close, looking westward to where the sun sent out final dying rays. In that fading light Duke took in all the land at a glance, sweeping his gaze all across the remote distance of the horizon. The face of his wife came to mind, generating the strange mixture of love, joy, and torment that her memory always brought.

Duke watched night fall like mist on the land. As the sun winked out in the west, he smiled vaguely.

"Charity."

"Yes, Pa?"

Duke stood, the mysterious smile on his face breaking into a full grin. He was gazing southward.

"Pa?"

"Hush, child—go back to the house and fix yourself up. And throw on a pot of beans. Tucker's been riding a long way, I expect, and likely he'll be hungry!"

If you enjoyed Cameron Judd's action-packed saga of the untamed American West, be sure to look for his next book, SNOW SKY, at your local bookstore. Cameron Judd is one of the most promising young writers in the field of Western adventure.

Here's an exciting preview of the next book by Cameron Judd

SNOW SKY

On sale in November 1990, wherever Bantam Books are sold.

Chapter 1

For the third night in a row, the man forced the boy up the mountail trail. The higher they climbed, the louder pealed the thunder and the harder fell the rain, driving down in bullets and drenching them as they ascended. The man's hat had long ago soaked through and now sluiced water off its down-turned brim and onto his wide shoulders.

Rain mixed with tears on the boy's face as the man roughly shoved him forward. "Go on, you," he said. The boy bit his lip and, as always, said nothing.

Narrower grew the trail. Finally the rain slackened, then all but stopped. Clouds drooping heavily from the gray sky formed a drizzling mist about the pair, and fog rose from the emptiness to their right, where the trail gave way to a sheer bluff. The boy's feet slid on the muddy path; twice he fell, and twice the man swore and pulled him up. They went on.

When the land disappeared before them and they finally stopped, they stood atop a high peak, looking down onto dark conifer treetops bending in the wind. Lightning flashed simultaneously with the man's wicked smile. He reached menacingly toward the cringing but still-silent boy . . .

Florida Cochran woke up with a scream. Man, boy and mountain melted into the smooth darkness of her bedroom wall.

Tudor Cockran, her husband, bolted up beside her. Florida turned her wide moon face with its watery blue eys on him; the moonlight was so bright through the window tonight that he could read the silent sorrow in her eyes.

"Same dream?" he softly inquired.

She nodded sadly.

"Flory, what am I going to do about you and your crazy dreams?" he asked, and then wished he hadn't, for he knew already what she wanted him to do. So far he had refused.

Someone approached the closed bedroom door quickly but unevenly; bare feet slapped, scraped against the oiled slab floor on the other side of the door.

"Mr. and Mrs. Cochran! Are you all right in there?"

Cochran called back, "Fine, fine, Reverend Viola. Flory just had that dream again." The inquirer in the hallway was a preacher who had been lodging in the Cochran Inn for two nights now, lingering to let a bruised foot heal before he continued on to Snow Sky. Both nights Flory had dreamed the same dream and screamed herself awake, and the tall, solemn clergyman had limped down to the door on his sore foot to make sure everything was all right.

The preacher padded arhythmically back to his room and Flory settled back into her feather pillow. For the next several minutes she sniffed and from time to time dabbed her eyes with the sheet, pretending to hide it so Cochran wouldn't notice while really making sure he did. Cochran listened for a while, then sighed and sat up on the bedside and reached down for his boots.

"It's a curse indeed for a grown man to have a bladder the size of a pea," he muttered. He pulled on his boots, fumbled around on the bedside lampstand for his spectacles, then walked out. An outhouse stood at the edge of the woods behind the inn, over near the stable where the horses and mules shifted about quietly in the moonlight. Cochran crossed the yard. It was a beautiful night blessed with a cool breeze that carried wonderful scents of earth and forest upon its shoulders.

As Cochran walked back toward the inn, he stopped to gaze thoughtfully at the moon. After a few moments he looked at the ground, shook his head, and inwardly surrendered, pondering the sacrifices men have to make to keep their women happy. Over the years he had made several for Flory, and was about to obligate himself to her for one more. But he didn't much mind it, not really. Flory's happiness was worth it.

She was still awake when he returned. He slipped off his boots, tucked his nightshirt down about his knees, and slid back beneath the covers.

"All right, Flory, you needn't bring it up again. I'll go after them," he said.

She sat up, surprised. "You mean it?"

"If you think you and Theon can run things here without me for a while, I do."

"Of course we can. Oh, Tudor, you're a wonderful man."

His back was toward her, but he felt her smile beaming on him like sunshine through a window. It was good to know she was happy again, especially after all the worry her dreams had brought her. Cochran wondered why he had fought the inevitable as long as he had, plumped his pillow, and went back to sleep.

Breakfast was salt pork and biscuits, the latter so hard that Cochran silently wondered if Flory had saved them from last Christmas. Flory had two main failings: she couldn't sing and she couldn't make biscuits, though she tried hard to do both, sometimes at the same time, which did not improve matters.

The Reverend P. D. Viola sat across the table from Cochran, shoveling big slabs of meat into his down-turned mouth and gulping coffee from a china cup. Between bites he was talking about Flory's dream, in which he appeared interested even while also seeming preoccupied and somber. He had said a time or two that he had a dreadful duty awaiting him in Snow Sky, but Cochran was not a busybody and did not pursue the matter, nor had he allowed Flory to do so.

"There is sometimes a symbolism in dreams," the preacher was saying to Cochran. "Of what does this dream consist?"

Cochran described the dream based on Flory's slightly vague descriptions.

Viola said, "An image, perhaps, of Abraham taking his son up the mountain to sacrifice him."

"I don't think that's it," Cochran responded wearily, not enjoying the subject. "The boy and man in the dream were in here a few days back. Came late, stayed one night, and left early. The man looked edgy and the boy never said a word. He just looked at Flory a few times in a way that made her worry for him. She's had the dream three nights straight. She feels like the man is going to do bad to the boy. I don't know where she gets her notions."

The preacher bit off a piece of biscuit so hard it crunched like a bone. "Despite what you say, I find the imagery remarkably biblical," he said. "But even if not, perhaps her dream is meaningful in some other way. The story of Joseph and his interpretation of dreams gives us verification that sometimes dreams are a vehicle of insight from above and from within."

Cochran didn't really understand all that and was ready to drop it anyway. He took a swig of coffee and another bite of biscuit. A moment later Flory came in from the kitchen, smiling at Cochran more brightly than she had since their honeymoon nineteen years before.

"Anyone need more eggs?" she asked. She brushed past Cochran and patted his shoulder lovingly.

"A delicious meal, ma'am, and I'm satisfied," Viola said. Cochran wondered how a preacher could voice such a lie; surely Viola had noticed the biscuits. Then again, maybe a grim fellow such as he enjoyed breaking his teeth. "A fine tableful to fit a man for a difficult encounter to come, and I'm about to go to one. My foot's in good enough condition, I believe, for me to travel on."

"My husband is to do some traveling, too," she said, looking at Cochran and smiling again. "You'll be pleased. He's going off to do a good deed."

"Oh?" The clergyman looked inquiringly at Cochran. "Where are you going?"

"Snow Sky," Flory answered for Cochran, who wished she hadn't, for he knew at once what would follow: a suggestion from either Viola or Flory that the two men travel together. Cochran had nothing against Viola except his overly serious manner. Cochran himself was prone to be serious, but the preacher did not look like he had smiled since childhood.

"You plan to leave innkeeping for mining?" Viola asked.

"No. I'm just going on an errand for my wife. Nothing, really," Cochran responded.

"He's going to help a young boy in trouble," Flory said proudly, still beaming at her husband.

The clergyman raised his brows. "The boy in the dream?"

"Tudor told you about that? Yes, the very one. Now, Reverend Viola, I don't claim any gift of secret vision, but I just know in my heart that poor boy is in trouble. Tudor is going to find him and make sure he's safe."

"I see." The preacher asked Cochran: "How do you know this man and boy are in Snow Sky?"

"Flory heard the man say something to the boy about Snow Sky. Besides, that's where everybody who travels this way is headed anymore."

"True. Speaking of travel, perhaps we could conduct ours together. I've been a bit melancholy, I admit, for I have already mentioned the unpleasant matter awaiting me in Snow Sky. A meeting with a person I dread encountering again. I could use a bit of good companionship on the road."

Cochran was glad he had seen that one coming. "I appreciate it, Reverend Viola, but I've already got a traveling partner." He shot a quick glance at Flory.

"Who?" Flory asked, surprised. She had thought he was going alone.

"Hiram Frogg," Cochran said.

Flory went dark as a snuffed candle. "If my husband intends to be in the company of Mr. Frogg, Reverend Viola, then you most assuredly do not want to travel with him," she said in a much cooler tone than before.

"Who is this Mr. Frogg?" Viola asked. "A strange name, Frogg."

"Just a friend of mine," Cochran responded.

"And a no-account of the worst sort," Flory added. "A common criminal. A thief and fighter—and he's been in jail."

"And got out again when his time was up," Cochran reminded his wife. "He's settled down a lot compared to what he used to be."

"He's settled, all right. Settled like an old hound too lazy to scratch his own fleas."

Flory had never liked Hiram Frogg, and had secretly hoped for a long time now that he would be lured away by the silver strikes at Snow Sky. So far, to her chagrin, he had not. Frogg was a most unambitious man, unattracted by anything that required labor. Frogg claimed to be a blacksmith, of all things, though he seldom actually worked. Flory suspected that her husband sometimes slipped Frogg money. He was soft like that, especially where Frogg was concerned.

Flory had never anticipated that Cochran was planning to take Frogg with him; she wondered if he had come up with the idea to get back at her for nagging him to make this trip. The fact was, Cochran actually hadn't considered taking Frogg until he realized a moment ago that he needed an out to keep from having to travel with Viola. The more he considered it, though, the notion of taking Frogg along seemed good. Frogg wasn't much for brains or appearance, but he was comfortable to travel with, able to take care of himself. He would be a good companion in a swarming new mining town.

Viola stood, smacked lips smeared with grease and salt, then wiped his mouth on his napkin. "I must be off. I shall pray travel mercies for you and Mr. Frogg," he said to Cochran. "I trust you shall do the same for me. Perhaps we shall see each other in Snow Sky, or you'll catch up with me on the trail."

"Maybe so," Cochran said. "Preacher, that little Bible in your pocket's about to fall out."

"Indeed it is," Viola said, tucking back into his shirt pocket a thin, red-backed New Testament. "Mrs. Cochran, I'll gather my things and return to settle my bill."

When he was gone, Flory said, "I'd much rather you travel with a Godly man than with a weasel like Toad Frogg."

Cochran bit off a piece of salt pork. "Don't call him Toad, Flory. You know that makes him mad."

Hiram Frogg leaned over and spat a brown stream of tobacco juice onto the ground. He was sitting on his anvil, which, Cochran had noted, was dusty and strung with cobwebs from lack of use.

Frogg wiped a trace of brown juice from his lower lip and nodded. "I might go with you at that," he said. "Though it all sounds a little difficult. You think you can find a man and boy in that town? Snow Sky had nearly three thousand folks, last I heard, and more coming every day."

"The point isn't so much to find them as just to try, so Flory will be satisfied," Cochran answered. "You're right—it's a lot of trouble for little enough reason, but if you had a woman you loved you'd know why I'm doing it.''

"What happens if you do find them?" Frogg asked, resettling his tobacco with his long tongue. That tongue, combined with his wide mouth, slightly bugged eyes, and unfortunate last name, were what had earned Frogg the nickname of Toad. But few dared call him that to his face, for he would fight anyone who did, friend or foe. His reputation as a brawler was one of many things Flory disliked about him.

Cochran shrugged. "I suppose I'll watch them and make sure the boy's all right. Maybe I'll talk to the man to see what his story is, if I think I need to. Mostly I just have to satisfy Flory the boy ain't been thrown off a cliff or something.''

"Sounds crazy.''

"No crazier than Flory will make me if I don't do it. She's thought of nothing else for days, and she won't let up about it. You see, Flory swears when that boy looked up at her while she was serving the table, she could see he was begging her for help. Begging with his eyes, Flory says, though he never said a word the whole time he was at the inn. Flory says something is wrong, that the man isn't the boy's father. And they didn't look at all alike, that's a fact.''

"Do you know their names?"

"Not the boy's. Man signed in as John Jackson."

"Sounds made up," Frogg said.

"The world's full of John Jacksons. Besides, a man can make up a name if he wants. A lot of them do out here.''

Frogg rose from his anvil and yawned. Some of the anvil's cobwebs clung to his dirty trousers. "Well, Tudor, I'll go with you, crazy and henpecked though you may be." He stretched. "I been wanting to get back to Snow Sky anyway, just to see how it's grown since the last time I was there.''

Cochran was glad to see Frogg had at least some

interest in Snow Sky. He had always thought that if Frogg could collect up even half a basketload of ambition he might head to the mining town to set up his business. He could make a good living if he did. Blacksmiths were much in demand in mining towns, and indeed one of the first acts of Snow Sky's governing body, according to a copy of the Snow Sky *Argus* somebody had recently left at the Cochran Inn, was to put out an offer of a free building and house for any good blacksmith. Lawyers, saloon keepers, gamblers, and soiled doves Snow Sky had aplenty; skilled artisans it sorely lacked. Frogg wasn't a high-quality blacksmith, maybe, but he was honest and could beat out a decent horseshoe when he had to. Cochran had showed the story in the *Argus* to Frogg, but Frogg had not reacted.

Cochran himself had thought briefly of opening an inn or hotel in Snow Sky, but had decided against it. He had worked too long and hard establishing this one, and as long as Snow Sky kept attracting travelers, he figured he would thrive sufficiently right where he was. His inn's location about a day and a half from the mining town made it an almost essential stopover for westbound travelers to Snow Sky.

"When do we leave?" Frogg asked.

"Today. Get your things together, and I'll be back around in a little while."

"You're too good to that woman, Tudor. Running off on a fool's errand just because she squalls in the night."

Cochran adjusted his spectacles and said, "You just ain't been in love with anybody, Frogg. You don't love nothing but cards and sleeping late."

Frogg snorted. "I been in love plenty. Ain't met the first dance hall gal yet I didn't fall in love with."

Back at the inn, Viola was long gone and Flory was already packing Cochran's bag and bedroll. Theon, the skinny, slow-witted young man who helped the Cochrans run the inn, was sweeping out the main room. "Sure wish you'd take me to Snow Sky," he said to Cochran.

"You're needed here," Cochran answered. "You're too important to spare."

Theon smiled at the flattery and swept a little harder.

Seeing his bedroll depressed Cochran, who hated sleeping on the ground. He wondered if that was why he had become an innkeeper—to do his part to keep the human race from having to sleep outdoors any more than necessary.

"Don't you let Toad Frogg get you into trouble," Flory instructed sternly.

"I ain't a little boy, Flory."

"No, but Toad is. I really hate that you're taking him with you. You could have done better. That preacher Viola seemed a nice enough man."

"I'm sure he is. But he had too much starch about him. Frogg you can relax with."

"Oh, I'm sure. His idea of relaxing is gambling and drinking and I don't want to think what else. Don't let him tempt you to go to some cheap crib harlot, you hear?"

"I'm not in the market for crib harlots," Cochran said.

"What's a crib harlot?" Theon asked as he swept.

"Flory'll explain it when I'm gone," Cochran answered, grinning as Flory shot him a harsh look.

But a moment later she came to her husband and put her arms around him. Her gruffness vanished and she spoke tenderly. "Thank you," she said. "That little boy needs help. I know it as well as I know my own name. You'll help him if you find him, won't you?"

Cochran said, "If he needs it . . ."

He started to say more, but she planted a big kiss on his mouth and blocked off the words.

Chapter 2

The first night on the ground went as badly as Cochran had feared. He awakened stiff and aching, thoroughly repentant for his decision to make this trip and angry at Flory for having pushed him to it. Frogg, meanwhile, was as cheerful as ever. He had already built a fire and was frying bacon and corncakes in a spider skillet.

"Morning, Tudor!" he said. "Beautiful day for riding!"

Cochran rose and stretched, wincing. "I hope they got a good hotel in Snow Sky."

"Oh, they got plenty of hotels, but nothing as good as your inn. That's the trouble with a new mining town. You got to settle for what you can get, pot luck all the way."

They ate breakfast silently. Three big cups of black coffee slowly brought Cochran back to life and washed the rust from his joints. By the time Frogg had rinsed out his skillet and poured off the dregs of the coffee pot. Cochran was in a much better humor, actually beginning to anticipate with some pleasure the visit to Snow Sky. After all, a man had to see different scenes now and again just to keep from becoming stagnated. Cochran wondered if maybe he already was that way; he normally moved around about as much as a farm pond, and saw little more excitement. Maybe the trip would do him good.

As they rode, Frogg talked about Snow Sky, which had been founded beneath an overcast sky the previous year, 1889, on a snowy February day. An idle comment by one of its founders about snowy sky stretching above gave the town an informal name that finally had become permanent.

The silver chlorides at Snow Sky had assayed out at promising levels, and new, even richer lodes of silver and quartz were discovered by the week. Before the summer of '89 had ended, Snow Sky was a full-scale mining camp with 25-cent beer and dollar-a-shot whiskey, flare-lighted streets, and scores of saloons, faro parlors, whorehouses and lawyers' offices.

"You see if it ain't the next Leadville," Frogg said. "The railroad's already scouting out a route for itself."

"If you think so highly of Snow Sky, how come you don't live there?" Cochran asked.

"Been thinking about that. Maybe I'll stay on this time, open me a smithy."

Now that Frogg was actually talking about becoming a more respectable citizen, Cochran suddenly had his doubts. Frogg wouldn't be able to keep at his work with a lot of recreational diversions close at hand, and Snow Sky had plenty. Minimal law to supervise them all, too, although Cochran had read, in that same copy of the *Argus*, that the town's merchants had banded together to appoint a marshal and a small police force, and had even built a jail.

The pair rode slowly but steadily almost half the day, not pushing the horses too hard, stopping twice to spell them. Cochran's mind had drifted away from the man and boy he was supposedly seeking, but when he and Frogg stopped about one o'clock for a meal he thought of them again, and wondered if perhaps Flory was right about the pair. She had good instincts, especially about children. Maybe she really had read a plea for help in the boy's eyes.

Then again, maybe it was just another case of Flory's feelings getting stirred up by the presence of a child. Cochran felt a pang. Flory's inability to give them children was a private wound they nursed together. Life was unfair; Flory would have made the finest of mothers.

They finished their beans and lay back beneath a tree to let them settle while the horses cropped the wild grasses. In a few moments Frogg was snoring with his hat pulled down over his eyes and his hands behind his head. Cochran, though, didn't nap; he got up after a few minutes and walked around, looking at the mountains with their evergreen slopes and barren expanses of stone made brilliant by the sunlight. A while later he went over and gently kicked Frogg awake, and they mounted up and continued.

A NOTE FROM THE AUTHOR

I was born in 1956 in Tennessee, the state in which I have lived all my life. I wrote my first western at age twenty-two and now I am writing exclusively for Bantam.

My interest in the American West is just part of a broader interest in the frontier. I am fascinated by the vast westward expanses on the other side of the Mississippi, but I am equally intrigued by the original American West: the area west of the Appalachians and east of the Mississippi. I hope someday to write fiction set in that older frontier at the time of its settlement, in addition to traditional westerns.

My interest in westerns was sparked in early childhood by television, movies, and books. I love both the fact of the West and the myth of the West; both aspects have a valid place in popular fiction.

I received an undergraduate degree in English and journalism, plus teaching accreditation in English and history, from Tennessee Technological University in 1979. Since that time I have been a newspaper journalist by profession, both as a writer and editor. Today I live near Greeneville, Tennessee, one of the state's most historic towns. Greeneville is the seat of the county that contributed one of America's original frontier heroes to the world—Davy Crockett. Greeneville was also the hometown of President Andrew Johnson and was for several years the capital of the Lost State of Franklin—an eighteenth-century political experiment that came close to achieving statehood.

My home is in rural Greene County. My wife, Rhonda, and I have three children, Matthew, Laura, and Bonnie.

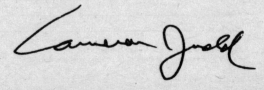